To Ethel —

With memories of our
early discovery of books together...
Uncle Welly's library, how wonderful
it was to me! Fondly
Ethel

THE
CHAPERONE

By Ethel Gordon

FREER'S COVE
THE CHAPERONE

THE
CHAPERONE

Ethel Gordon

Coward, McCann & Geoghegan
New York

I

1

I RECEIVED MISS MILLICENT WALDRON's letter on the last day of school. It was the day of the annual farewell party for the faculty of the Burns Junior College for Women, and the Burns sisters who owned and headed the school had acceded to the times at last and allowed gin to be served. I'd had two martinis, but by the time I reached my apartment the elation of the alcohol was evaporating, my head was pounding, and my spirits were unaccountably low.

It should have been the reverse. I should have been pitched high with excitement. It was the end of the term, my vacation had begun, and I was going to France for the whole summer to paint. I seemed to have a sense rather of things ending than beginning; another year had passed and—and nothing had happened. I was a year older, turning twenty-eight, Carrie Belding, art teacher, would-be artist, tall, on the bony side, brown straight hair, brown eyes, not in love, and with no one in love with me. No wonder I felt low. Sometimes I had the feeling that I was always waiting, waiting, for the breakthrough in my painting when I would take the giant step from proficiency to significance, for the breakthrough in my emotions when I would find myself plunged into passion. Maybe the two were tied together, maybe the fault was in me, and neither would come until I broke through myself.

Well. I unlocked the door and let myself in. I live in a loft building that has been converted into living quarters in a rundown section of lower Manhattan. I pay for the luxury of space rather more than the miserable, seedy street warrants, but I don't like to shut myself up in a box at night, I want the walls to be far away. I whitewashed the apartment myself; the windows on the street side go from floor to ceiling, and they are bare except for the canvas shades which I lower at night, which I made myself, too. I have straw mats on the dark-painted floor, and a mattress on a platform for a bed which is covered during the day with a piece of bright Indian cotton. I have a drafting table to eat on, and two white wicker chairs from the veranda of my parents' house in Dorset, Vermont, that I brought here after my mother sold the place and moved west with her new husband. But there is a dazzle of color from my paintings, on the walls and stacked alongside them. Sometimes I think the apartment is like my life, spare and austere, and then there are those paintings that seem to spring from my brush, which make me think there is another Carrie Belding inside this one, waiting to step forward. All this is preliminary; at any moment the change will come, the breakthrough, I am ready, only— Only why is it taking so long?

The trustees of the Burns Junior College did not come across with the vacation bonus that was whispered about the last month of the term. Hard times was the excuse, we must all tighten our belts a little, and after all, teachers do have that lovely summer vacation to enjoy, ten whole weeks of it. I can almost hear the trustees justifying their withholding it as they lounge at their white pool houses in the Caribbean or on the decks of their yachts in the Aegean. Most of our trustees are alumnae of Burns Junior College, which draws its students from the most prestigious families in America. You would think they would remember their school days and their teachers with nostalgia and bonuses, and to do them justice they often do, but the market is fluctuating now, I read, and so no bonuses, and it will be a question if I can cover the cost of even the most spartan summer abroad. I have managed to save my air fare and the money to rent a small car, but even the poorest excuse for a room is now expensive. So, if I can't afford a room every night, I told myself, I'll simply sleep in the back seat of my car.

Inexplicably the thought, coupled with the last of the gin left in me, made me kick off my shoes with abandon. One of them sailed off and hit the wall which is the common one between my half of the loft and the half occupied by Peter Wilencz. Peter is from Nebraska, and his family is Polish, or Czech; he is tenderhearted, and worries about my loneliness. Sometimes we knock on the wall and he comes to my place or I go to his, and we drink coffee or wine together. He has many friends, but I think he would love me if only I could love him. My shoe must have seemed like a signal to him, because almost at once, to my dismay, he was at my door.

He grinned at me. He is muscular and balding, with merry eyes.

"Are you all right, Carrie?" He sounded very sober, the

way sober people sound to people who have been drinking.

"I think so," I said doubtfully.

"I came over to tell you I made that Greek stew you said you liked the other time. And I've got a bottle of wine. I thought you might want to celebrate your vacation starting." He hesitated. He said, "We could go out to dinner, if you wanted."

I wished dining with Peter would seem more like a celebration. I shook my head. "I'm not up to eating. I'm not even sure I can stay awake. I think the best thing for me is to get into bed and sleep until my plane leaves next week."

"Want some company?" He was suddenly serious.

"I wouldn't be any good, Peter. I'd go right to sleep."

I've sensed before that he wouldn't mind making love to me, I don't know why; he has so many beautiful girls whom I would sometimes meet on their way to his room. He's a photographer, and I suppose he has a chance to meet them in his work. Maybe he wanted to make love to me out of kindness, maybe he thought love was what I needed, the dead tree struck to burgeoning life. No, that was morbid. I am not a dead tree, just slow to blossom, or maybe I've not found what is needed to blossom.

"Sure?"

"Sure, Peter."

I let him out and locked the door. I slipped off my clothes and got between the sheets. The sun was setting, it was June, and hot, and after a while I threw off the sheet. My thoughts drifted. Had I disgraced myself at the party? Probably not; in spite of the other Carrie Belding who would act any way she pleased, this one was well disciplined. Just before the party ended I had a hazy memory of one of the Misses Burns kissing me on the cheek. "Enjoy your summer, see you next September," she had said, which she would not have said if I'd disgraced myself. Burns is an impeccable school for impeccable young women. There's the usual percentage of pot smokers and occasionally a girl is discovered on pills or even heroin, and now and then one drops out, pregnant, but on the whole these matters are handled discreetly. The faculty is almost as impeccable, daughters of alumnae or daughters of friends who need the money, and a trustee can be telephoned who will put in a good word with the Burns sisters.

That happens to be how I got my job. Miss Millicent Waldron, one of the trustees, used to spend her summers in Dorset where my father grew up. When I had to find a job teaching after I graduated from Bennington, because my father and mother couldn't stake me indefinitely while I tried to make it as a painter, it was my father who asked me if I wanted him to write to Miss Waldron. To our surprise, she wrote back, having arranged an interview for me with the Misses Burns.

I was engaged, although I never did meet Miss Waldron. She never asked to see me, though I wrote her a nice thank-you note. At the last faculty art show someone told me she had noticed a painting of mine and inquired about me, and I was sure she would buy it, but she never did.

I wished she had bought the painting. It would have made the summer a lot more comfortable. I wished the board of trustees had voted us a bonus, so I could have stayed in Paris for a little while. I wished I loved Peter so I could have let him keep me company in bed. I wished I loved . . . I thought about our house in Dorset when I was a girl before my father died and my mother remarried, and I remembered my father coming home from school in the snow and stamping his galoshes on the wooden boards of the porch to get the snow off, so that the house trembled. I thought about Henry Benoit whom I had loved in high school, and about Dick Maidman who went to the University of Vermont when I was in Bennington and who was the only boy who had ever made love to me. Hot tears rolled down through my closed eyes, the gin, I suppose. I am not cold by nature, or abnormally selective; it's just that I think I will know from somewhere deep inside me when it will be the man I will want, and it hasn't happened, not even with Dick Maidman . . .

I slept.

I awoke, and it was night. The streetlamps shone through bluishly into the loft. I was clearheaded and hungry. I threw on slacks and a shirt, and found some Genoa sausage in the icebox, and tomatoes, and milk. Padding around on the cool floor, eating my sandwich, I saw the letter at my feet.

Someone, Peter maybe, had seen it sticking out of my box and pushed it under the door. The envelope was such handsome vellum I thought it must be a wedding invitation. Before I opened it I finished my sandwich and milk and wiped my hands. How could I have guessed that its contents would change the course of my life?

When I turned it over I saw the name in raised letters without ink. Millicent Waldron, and a Madison Avenue address. Miss Waldron! She had made up her mind about the painting and she was going to buy it. I had priced it impulsively at three hundred dollars. Three hundred dollars would pay for my meals for the whole summer. My hands beginning to tremble, I ripped open the envelope.

"Dear Miss Belding," said the letter. "I have been debating

for several days whether or not I might approach you on a rather delicate and confidential matter."

My first reaction was: so it wasn't the painting after all.

"I trust it is not presuming on our slight acquaintance. I feel remiss about not having been in touch with you after your father's letter and your employment at Burns."

So she had not forgotten her favor to me.

"Will you come to see me on the evening of the fourteenth of June, at eight o'clock?" the letter went on. "My niece Maria will be at the theater at that time, and I do not want her to be present when we talk. I shall expect you, unless I hear to the contrary. Thank you. Yours truly, Millicent Waldron."

Two things struck me. It had the overtones of a command rather than a request in its imperiousness. I remember my father saying to me, before he wrote his letter to Miss Waldron, "Don't forget, there are many people, even people of importance, who feel that a favor given is like a credit in the bank, from which the donor may draw at some time."

Maybe Millicent Waldron was drawing on her credit on the fourteenth of June.

And the second fact that followed hard on the first was that the very pretty blond girl in my second period class was Miss Waldron's niece. I don't know why I hadn't made the connection between Maria Waldron and her aunt, except that five years had gone by since I came to Burns and I had allowed myself to forget Millicent Waldron, and besides, Waldron is a fairly common name.

So Maria Waldron was her niece. I couldn't help but notice her in class because she was much prettier than the others, in an Alice in Wonderland sort of way, small and rounded, with guileless blue eyes and an upturned nose. Why should she be a matter of concern to her aunt? She was an average student. My class was well attended, even popular, and there was little cutting. Most of the girls enjoyed putting oils on canvas and drawing with colored chalks, and for the most part turned out passable efforts. In five years of teaching I've encountered only one or two genuine talents, and Maria was certainly not one of them.

If it had been about Maria's classwork, Miss Waldron would have arranged an interview through the Burns sisters, and I could imagine no need for secrecy. Private tutoring? No need for secrecy there either. Besides, I wasn't available for tutoring; all my classes knew I was flying to Europe this summer. They had all chipped in to buy me a handsome red cosmetic case which I had no use for.

It must be something else.

I couldn't have gone to bed now, even if I hadn't already napped. For a while I tried working on a canvas, but I was too distracted for work. And not ready for sleep. It was after midnight but I let myself out of my apartment so I could walk off my restlessness.

My friends at Misses Burns think I am crazy to walk the deserted streets of downtown Manhattan in the middle of the night, but I haven't learned to be afraid. I carry a heavy over-the-shoulder bag I could swing at an attacker, but so far I have never tested it to see how effective it would be. Now and then a derelict of a man will shuffle out of the darkness and ask me for a quarter, or a whiskey-laden breath will wheeze something about having a little fun. But the voice and the face suggest nothing but sadness.

Sometimes I have wondered if I am not really asking for

something to happen to me, something that will shake and even shatter me, and put me together in a way that is closer to the Carrie Belding I might really be. Does Miss Waldron's letter hint of some adventure? Might she not offer me a new life? I picture her, wise and beautiful, telling me sternly, "Why are you wasting your talent on those prosaic little girls? Go away, Tahiti, the Hebrides, Madagascar, paint, devote yourself to your art. I will give you the money...."

And later that night, in my bed, in the moments before sleep took over, when reasonable thoughts burst apart like the patterns in a kaleidoscope, I thought of a mad, inexplicable adventure, and an adventurer, dark, powerful, even unscrupulous, who would take me along with him . . .

Grow up, I told myself, drifting at last into sleep.

2

On the evening of June fourteenth I was too impatient to sit in my flat and wait for eight o'clock, so I started out early to walk to the Madison Avenue address. The air was warm and hazy and smelled of gasoline, but I did not mind. It smelled like a summer dusk in New York, and seemed to underline the fact that it was vacation and I would be leaving by the end of the week.

My timing was perfect. Walking leisurely had brought me to her neighborhood just at eight o'clock. I began checking numbers. The number on the envelope corresponded to the number on a red stone Renaissance palace with a courtyard, with iron brackets on the walls like on the palaces of the Medici. The only incongruous note was the air conditioners installed in the windows.

So, every day Maria Waldron emerges in her blue jeans and long Alice in Wonderland hair from this splendor and gets into a black limousine and is driven to my class where she patiently dabs paint like all the other girls. I was impressed in spite of myself. I resisted the impulse to pound on the brass-studded door with the giant brass lion's head knocker, and rang the bell instead. A servant admitted me.

"I'm Miss Belding. Miss Waldron is expecting me." I held the envelope in my hand, in case she would not believe me.

"Please come in," she said. I followed her across a marble floor into a dim room where among shelves of books in leather bindings an air conditioner hummed comfortably. I sat erect in a deep leather chair, an Oriental rug in faded reds and blues under my feet, and I felt as if I were waiting to be interviewed for the position of upstairs maid. Five minutes later a figure appeared, blocking the doorway.

"How do you do, Miss Belding," wheezed an elderly voice. A short, stout woman hobbled in, supporting herself on two canes. I stood up to shake hands, but her hands were occupied with lowering herself carefully and deliberately onto a straight-backed chair. She breathed a noisy sigh of relief. One of her canes fell down. I reached to pick it up, but she motioned me to let it lay. She was wearing something flowered, and a double strand of large pearls was partly lost in the fat of her neck.

"How is your father?"

"He had cancer. He died five years ago."

"A pity," she said. "Such a nice man. We would walk together and he would tell me the names of rocks he found. Summers were lovely in Dorset." But she seemed preoccupied, as if these preliminaries were necessary but must be gone through as quickly as possible. When I murmured something about the house, she frowned. "It belonged to my brother. It's far too large for me now. Such a nuisance to get around since I have become crippled. Arthritis. I installed an elevator, but I am in constant fear I will fall on those damn marble floors."

There was nothing more to say.

She began abruptly. "Miss Belding, let me get to the point of your visit. I am only comfortable sitting for a very limited time. Besides, if the musical is boring Maria might take it into her head to leave early, and I am most anxious to talk to you alone. She knows I've written to you, and I've told her a lie, that the only time you could make it was tonight. However, I'm sure she understands why I don't want her to hear what we are saying."

I could only nod.

She remembered her position as hostess. "May I offer you some sherry? Iced tea? Lemonade?"

I shook my head. I was too taut with curiosity to swallow anything.

She sucked in her breath. "Maria is my brother's child. My brother appointed me her guardian. She is seventeen, or is it eighteen? No, not quite. When she is twenty-one, she will come into a considerable amount of money."

I nodded again. Maria was like most of the girls at Burns. Most of them, except our token scholarship students, would come into considerable amounts of money. I suppose I should have acted more impressed; for some reason it was important to Miss Waldron that I be impressed.

She sounded piqued as she went on: "Maria will be extraordinarily wealthy when she is twenty-one, Miss Belding.

She is an only child, the child of her father's old age. Her mother, who was considerably younger, received a large divorce settlement, and has had little to do with Maria. She married a Venezuelan and lives in Caracas. All my brother's estate goes to Maria. Even now the allowance he provided her is enough to support most families. I disagreed most emphatically when he told me how much, I thought it in bad taste, but my brother doted on her foolishly, and was determined to lavish on her in death what he would have had he lived."

She watched my face.

"You must realize that Maria's fortune would be very attractive to an unscrupulous man."

"Oh, yes," I said.

"Well, then," she said with another gusty sigh. We had reached the nugget of her story. "You remember that last year the Misses Burns sponsored a summer in Neuchâtel, where the girls could perfect their accents. I am told that the French spoken in Neuchâtel is as pure as any in France. Maria went. At the end of the summer the girls were given two weeks for travel, with a teacher. Maria elected to go with a group to Cannes. They chose a route through the mountains because it was less crowded and more scenic, and spent the night near a village called Belan-les-hauts. The hotel was called La Ferme, because it was once a farmhouse. It was cheap. Young people don't mind, and the school makes more money."

She looked at me as accusingly as if I had profited from the scheme. I mumbled something about the way of the world.

"I have been in touch with the teacher who went with them. She says the school used La Ferme for the last few years, ever since it was operated as a hotel. She says it is old but quite adequate, and run by Americans, two brothers. Or, one brother is American, the other half. She says most of the girls enjoy the experience. The isolation. Apparently Maria did, too. Only too much so. She insisted on staying there her entire two weeks instead of going on to Cannes."

She paused.

"It can be appealing to girls, the isolation, an ancient farmhouse—" I began.

She lifted a fat hand. "I'm not such a fool. Maria is interested neither in isolation nor in any form of architecture, ancient or otherwise. Of course there was a young man."

"Of course," I said. I should have thought of it myself.

"It was the younger brother, the one who is part French. Maria says he is out of sight, which means I believe that he is very attractive. Since she returned last fall they have been in constant communication, letters, packages. Even his friends come here and give her his personal greetings. And now she wants to spend the summer there with him, in that hotel."

I could not see why she was confiding in me. Did she think I had any influence over Maria, that I might persuade her not to go?

"She thinks she loves this young man," said Miss Waldron.

"It's possible."

"Maria is a birdbrain."

Maria is guileless and pretty, but that did not make her a birdbrain necessarily. I told this to Miss Waldron. I said, "It's easy to underestimate a girl when she's so pretty. One tends not to look deeper. But I think Maria is intelligent enough to know what she wants."

Her voice was sharper, as if she did not like being contradicted. "She is like her mother," she said. "Her mother also knew what she wanted, and how to get it. She was a size four, but as unswerving as a juggernaut when it came to marrying my brother's fortune. I am sure Maria loves him, or thinks she does. I don't question that. What concerns me is, does he love her?"

She did not let me attempt to answer.

"As I took the trouble to explain, Maria's money is well known. Do you think this young man has overlooked the fact? He hasn't even a university degree. No profession. He is a nobody. He helps his brother run that broken-down old hotel, that is all. During the winter Maria tells me he works at various luxury hotels in Europe, learning how to be a hotelkeeper, she says. He is very smooth and sophisticated, she says, manners that he has picked up in his hotel training, no doubt. Is it possible that a handsome and sophisticated man would love Maria for herself alone?"

"She's very pretty—"

"She is a child, and a birdbrain."

"Men love pretty girls, even birdbrains."

"But how is one to really know?" she said slowly, her eyes narrowing under their lizardlike folds of flesh.

I was silent.

"I would like to meet him," she said. "I would like to confront him, talk to him. I think I would know fairly soon. But Maria says he cannot come here, he is too busy. I think she is afraid for me to meet him. She knows I cannot travel. In a week I leave for Seal Harbor. I am taken in a wheelchair to the plane, and once at my house there I go nowhere until it is time for me to be flown back. Walking is too much for me. Even sitting requires all my strength. I cannot rely on

Maria's judgment, obviously. I need someone's eyes to report to me."

"There are discreet private investigators—" When I was a girl I watched *Perry Mason* on TV.

"I am not interested in what a private investigator would tell me. That the boy is poor? That he is handsome and hardworking? That the hotel just manages to survive? No. I am interested in something more subtle, something I could detect, something a mature, sensitive woman could detect. What does he really feel for Maria? If he is sincerely in love with her, if he is not a fortune hunter, I would not oppose her. Who knows, an early marriage might be right for her. I am selfish enough to want to turn the responsibility over to some upstanding man who could take care of her. But I owe it to my dead brother to see that what happened to him does not happen to his daughter."

What could I say but that I understood her predicament? The silence lengthened. Uncomfortably I blurted out what I suppose I should have said sooner, "I wish I could help you—"

Her glance was rapier fast, for all the fat. "Do you mean that?"

I retired, vaguely frightened. "What could I do?"

"You could go to La Ferme in my place."

I stared.

She spoke rapidly, "When Maria first came to me with her summer plans I said no, not unless she went with someone I knew. But none of her friends would spend a whole summer in a desolate place like that. She cried. Like her mother, she will have her way. I weakened. I said, there must be someone who could use a little extra money, someone who was artistic, who might find La Ferme interesting. She herself thought of you. She said you were going to France to paint. She said you were nice. You were somewhat different, she said. She thought you might be able to use the money."

I flushed, and thought Miss Waldron rather rude. After all, my family was as good as the Waldrons, even if they hadn't any money.

She must have noted my bristling. Subtly she proceeded to remind me of my debt.

"I have never mentioned to Maria my part in your obtaining your job. I would prefer that you keep it to yourself, too. She might think you felt under some obligation to me, which of course you need not; it was a pleasure to do it for your father."

But I did not want to spend the summer with Maria Waldron. All year I yearned to get away from the atmosphere of the classroom; anyone who has ever taught knows how important a complete break is, and being with Maria was not my idea of freedom.

Miss Waldron was saying, "I know that La Ferme is not the place you might choose to spend two months. A week perhaps. On the other hand, painters like Cézanne have painted those very mountains for years—"

"It isn't that, Miss Waldron. I'm sure I would find enough there to interest me for the summer, but—"

"Miss Belding," she said, proceeding full steam, "I will pay your fare, I will pay your hotel bill at La Ferme including your bar tabs, and I will give you a hundred dollars a week for writing me now and then to keep me informed."

I admit to being shaken. I said slowly, "There's something else. I'm not sure I can do what you want. I'm not a spy. Or a policeman, and even if I could be, I'm sure I wouldn't like it."

She said disdainfully, "I told you already I am not interested in that kind of information."

"I couldn't keep her . . . him . . . them—"

She cut short my stammerings. "I don't imagine for a moment you could keep them from getting into bed together, if they wish to. I could not myself, if I were there, any more than I can anticipate what she will do when she is out on a date. If she wants to, I will not stop her. No. I want your eyes, that is all, your awareness, your judgment as a sensitive woman. Would he marry her if she were penniless? She will confide in you if she trusts you, and she herself will tell you of her doubts. She will want to talk to someone, someone who has known love, and can discuss it with her."

Do I really know, myself? But I had no time for such thoughts. I was beginning to realize the full import of Miss Waldron's offer. All my expenses paid, and money besides. I could fly to Switzerland next winter to ski. Put a down payment on a used car to take me out of the city to paint. And as she put it, it was not an unpleasant or an unwholesome role she was asking me to play. I will be an observer, I will report my personal feelings. And as she said, that stony massif has been the choice of many painters, not only Cézanne.

"Remember," said Miss Waldron, "I am asking you to help her, not to hurt her, to act *in loco parentis,* as it were. I am sure you would not want to see her duped, or deceived."

"No, of course not—"

She was plainly tired, and her breathing sounded very labored in the quiet room. My hesitancy must have been exasperating. She flung it out, as a last tasty morsel she had been withholding: "And incidentally, that painting of yours at the faculty show. I have already expressed my pleasure in it to Miss Alethea Burns. I have been planning to buy it, but with all this worry about Maria— Three hundred, wasn't it?"

It was out-and-out bribery. I mumbled, "Do you really like it?"

"Charming," she said, "positively charming. I thought it might go in my bedroom. Yes, I have practically made up my mind about it."

I took a deep breath. "I would like very much to help you, Miss Waldron—"

She didn't wait any further. "Good. You'll go, then. Thank you very much, my dear. I have been sitting too long and my back is stiff. Will you reach me my canes? I must go to my room."

I helped her settle onto her canes. I followed her out to the hall. The same servant who had admitted me had just ushered in a sallow young man in a thick pullover.

Miss Waldron fixed her eyes on him.

The servant hurried over. "He's come for the package, ma'am. The one that was sent to Miss Maria."

"Well, give it to him then," she snapped ungraciously, and lowered herself into a kind of seat that hung over the banister on the marble stairway. She addressed herself to me as if the young man were not there.

"I want to hear your first impressions. First impressions are always important. You must write them down and send them to me as soon as you arrive."

She pressed a button, and the seat mounted slowly upward, carrying her with it. I said hurriedly, "When does Maria want to leave? And what arrangements—"

The elevated seat stopped on the fifth step. "Maria will

come to see you tomorrow. She will bring a check for the painting. All your bills will be sent to me."

Again she began to ascend with monumental ponderousness. "Dreadful to be incapacitated, dreadful," her voice floated down to me. "Thank you, Miss Belding, and goodbye. I hope you have a pleasant summer."

The door was open, the servant had just let out the young man with his package, and she held it open for me. I was out on Madison Avenue; ahead of me I could see the young man. He seemed hesitant about his direction. I wondered if he were foreign, and a stranger, and whether I should overtake him and offer him help.

Suddenly, close to me, I heard running feet. I have always wondered how I would behave if I thought myself pursued on the city streets, about to be attacked, robbed, or mugged. Now I know. Without looking behind me I bolted, sprinting blindly across the street in the direction of a lighted coffee shop.

Breathing hard in the safety of the doorway, I turned. There was only silence. Had I imagined it? No, there on the sidewalk I'd run away from lay the man's body; I could see his white pullover in the dimly lit street. I didn't stop to think, but ran back to him.

He was already sitting up, rubbing his shoulder.

"Are you hurt?"

He shook his head.

The package he had been carrying was gone.

"Your package! He must have stolen it!"

He began to curse in what I think was French, but accented.

"Shall I telephone the police from the coffee shop?"

But he had scrambled to his feet and without even a thank

you for my offer of help he took himself off hurriedly and disappeared around the corner.

I stared after him. But only for a moment. Well, this is New York, or the way everyone tells me New York is. I was sufficiently shaken to treat myself to the luxury of a taxi home, and driving downtown I was troubled by a recurring thought. Am I the mature woman Miss Waldron assumes I am? Will I be able to recognize love? Can I help Maria, if I have not been able to love, myself?

3

The buzzer from the hall below woke me in the morning. I pressed the button to release the locked door, and just managed to wash my face and pull on a shift before there was a rap outside. Whoever it was had negotiated those three flights with lightning speed.

It was Maria.

"Hi, Miss Belding. We didn't wake you, did we?" Behind her an elderly man in a chauffeur's uniform was rounding the last set of stairs. "It's after ten, and Aunt Millie said you'd be expecting us."

I ushered them in. She flung herself onto my unmade bed. He remained standing, catching his breath.

"Haywood is here for the painting."

"Oh." Miss Waldron was binding her bargain with dispatch. I found the canvas among those stacked completed paintings ranged along the wall; it was of skaters in the Rockefeller Center rink, and the huge tree glittering with ornaments and lights that had stood there during Christmas was in the background. "Shall I put some paper around it?"

"Don't bother. Woody will take good care of it. I'm not going back with you, Woody. I'm meeting friends for lunch and I'll taxi home."

Haywood put the painting under his arm and handed me an envelope. I slipped it into my pocket feeling unreasonably ashamed, as if I had taken a bribe.

The door closed behind him. "It's a darling picture," said Maria. "Aunt Millie told me I could have it for my room."

Miss Waldron had thought it might go in her bedroom, or so she had told me last night. It hadn't been worth the effort to pretend a serious interest in my painting, not even for a day. I suppose I was brooding over the way I had snatched at her bait. I suppose I was still smarting over the ignominy of my position, and how shrewdly she had guessed I would feel not only in her debt but that I would need the money. I could have said no to Miss Waldron, I am sure she would not have had me fired, and so I was wrong to resent the position she had put me in. But the painting hurt. The rich can be so arrogant, even when they are dispensing largesse. It takes so little sometimes to shield the feelings of others. Perhaps Miss Waldron thought three hundred dollars was enough soothing syrup—

Maria must have noticed my chagrin. She said with the shrewdness I had suspected might lie under her smooth oval face, "Did Aunt Millie buy the painting to make sure you were on her side?"

I said shortly, "If she did, she bought it for nothing."

"You're angry, Miss Belding."

I took a deep breath, and cleared away my thoughts. "If I am, I shouldn't be. Your aunt has been very fair."

"She has the most awful taste, anyway. You wouldn't *want* her to like your painting, Miss Belding. The only kind of painting she likes has someone in the family in it, draped in satin and wearing emeralds."

I had just read in the Sunday Travel Section of the *Times* about an English peer who was criticized for taking in paying guests at his ancestral estate. His remark to his critics was, "I never blush when I am making money." I repeated the words out loud to Maria with a kind of defiance.

She looked at me seriously. "It's funny you should say that, Miss Belding. You don't look as if you would care that much about money."

"Everyone cares about money if he hasn't any."

The expression on her face continued unexpectedly sober.

"Some things are much more important," she said. "I'm sure you believe that, Miss Belding. You have to, being the sort of person you are."

And suddenly I knew what she was driving at, her handsome young man at La Ferme. I felt ashamed of myself. "I was just being cynical. Maybe I was thinking of your aunt Millie."

"If I thought you were in the least like Aunt Millie I would never have asked her to speak to you about coming with me this summer. It's very important that you don't have her ideas. Honestly, she thinks that's all people think about, money."

The strange thing is that money has never seemed that attractive to me. When Edna Barry, who teaches biology at Burns, introduced me to her brother Sydney, who is a broker on Wall Street, it could have been a perfect arrangement for us. He liked the thought of my being an artist, and I knew I could have a good life with him. Besides, he was good-look-ing, and very sweet. Still, it seemed wiser not to continue seeing him, because I didn't think I would ever change. I said, "It's very nice to have, as long as you have the other things, the things that really matter, too."

She brightened. "That's just the way I feel, Miss Belding!"

"But it's inevitable that your aunt Millie worry about you. A large fortune is hard to ignore."

She studied me, her forehead furrowed. She said slowly, "Do you think it's possible that someone would fall in love with me even if I were poor?"

She was quite serious. And all at once for me she became just a young girl, not an heiress, a girl with all the doubts I had myself at her age, and maybe still do, all too human. Because even though she was so remarkably pretty, how would she ever be sure? No matter how convincing a man was, no matter how hard she wanted to believe him, would she ever rid herself of that last nagging doubt? I felt a sudden rush of pity, and affection.

"Maria, you'd have men falling all over themselves for you even if you didn't have a dime."

I think she felt the change in my voice. She came over to me and kissed me. "You're a honey, Miss Belding. I always knew you were."

I said briskly, so she would not know how touched I was, "It's Carrie. If we're going to spend the whole summer to-gether, let's not be so formal. I'll seem very forbidding to your friend at La Ferme if you treat me like your teacher."

Color washed up into her face. "Of course Aunt Millie told you about Egan."

"Egan? Is that his name?"

"Egan Jarret. His father was French. His mother was American." She fell silent, thoughtful, her color still high. "What did she tell you about him?"

"Only that he and his brother run this hotel. That you are attracted to him. She didn't have to tell me that. I'd guess it myself, otherwise why spend a summer at La Ferme, which she says is old and I gather less than adequate, and in a very out-of-the-way place."

"I'd stay in a hole, to be with Egan," she said.

Well, she was seventeen going on eighteen, and so she could say things like that, but I think I envied her a little and wished I could feel that way about someone.

"When you see Egan, you'll know why," she said. "That's going to be soon, I hope. It isn't that he's just handsome, and he is, terribly handsome. It's something else. It's the way he looks at me—" She stopped, and gave a little shiver. "But you'll see."

"What does he do, when he's not helping his brother at the hotel?"

"I'm sure Aunt Millie told you he does nothing," she said. "She has him down in her books as someone just out to marry a rich wife so he'll never have to work again. It isn't that way at all. His mother died when he was going to Cornell. His brother was made his guardian. That's Conor. Conor is a lot older, and an engineer, and his mother left the estate for Conor to manage. I suppose she thought he was very sensible, but he lost all the money she left him in some get-rich-quick scheme, and of course Egan couldn't continue with college. He felt he had to help Conor with his converting La Ferme into a hotel. It was their house, before."

"His brother is American?"

She nodded. "They have different fathers. Conor is Conor Macklyn."

"Then what are they doing running a hotel in France?"

"The property at Belan-les-hauts was all they had left after Conor lost all their money. They couldn't sell it. Who would buy it? It's in such a godforsaken place. But it has lots of bedrooms, and the taxes are high, so Conor thought they might run it as a hotel and maybe sell it that way. Egan works at different hotels in Europe during the winter so he can learn how hotels are operated. His brother is absolutely hopeless, though he's an engineer and he's very good at things like plumbing and wiring and fixing the stonework."

"Do they get along? I mean, does Egan resent his brother for losing his money?"

"Oh, no! Egan isn't that way at all. Egan adores Conor, and I will say for Conor, although he's barely civil to people, that he is very fond of Egan. Egan says that one of the reasons Conor's so very grim and unpleasant is that he's full of guilt for what he did to Egan. Conor is going to try and build up the hotel so it can be sold, and then he's going to give all the money to Egan, to make it up to him, at least partly."

She jumped off my bed as she talked, as if merely talking about Egan made her restless and eager to be on her way.

"When do you think you could be ready to go, Carrie?"

"All I have to do is defrost the refrigerator and lock the door. I had intended to leave by the end of the week."

"I have to buy some clothes. I mean"—again the wash of pink—"Egan and I will be free in the evening to go out together, and I'll want . . . some pretty things."

I wondered about my own wardrobe. Traveling as I had expected to do on my own involved mainly serviceable slacks and shirts that I could dry on a hanger over the bathtub. "Will I need to get dressed up at La Ferme?"

She burst out laughing. "Wait till you see it. It's a dungeon of a place, and no one stays there any longer than he has to. But maybe you'll be going in to Cannes or Nice so you better take something nice."

She gathered up her purse and jacket.

"I'm sure I could be ready by Monday, Carrie. Could you?"

Monday was fine.

"I'll call you as soon as I know the exact time the plane leaves," she said. "It *is* going to be great, isn't it, Carrie? I mean, you'll have your painting, and all, and I'll"—she laughed again—"I'll have Egan."

She ran down the steps. I came back into the flat and closed the door. Perhaps it would be great, after all, in spite of Miss Millicent Waldron. Or maybe because of Miss Waldron, at least partly. It would be nice to go shopping with money in my pocket for a change. I hurried to straighten up my room, unfamiliar thoughts of long flowing skirts and open sandals in my head. How could I think it would be anything but great, a long summer in France?

II

~

~

~

1

I WAS WAITING when the black car with Haywood driving parked in my street. Haywood came up to take my bag and my painting gear to the car. I cast a backward glance at the flat, the shades drawn, breathless in the heat, a sheet over my bed, and then I locked the door and slipped the key under Peter's door.

We had said good-bye last night. He had insisted on taking me to dinner at a Turkish restaurant where there was dancing and we had drunk too much wine. We had kissed, because I was stirred by wine and affection, and I felt sorry for him having to go to work the next morning, but I did not let him come into my flat as he wanted to because I did not entirely trust myself and wine and affection might be more persuasive than I knew. In the clear light of today I knew he would find someone else to console him for my absence.

At the lounge in the airport Maria's friends were waiting for her, some of whom I recognized from school. The boys looked attractive, and I wondered what Egan was like to make him so superior to them. It would have been so much simpler, and Miss Waldron would no dou' be pleased to have any one of them date Maria. Well, peo; were strange, and they were driven in ways inexplicable to anyone else. I am sure my mother would not have understood my breaking off with Sydney, and might have even thought in my position I should consider Peter. He might seem a little offbeat to her, but then I wasn't getting any younger.

I was glad to get on the plane. I was tired of being talked to politely as Miss Belding, teacher. I wanted to cast aside all associations with the workday world. I remember the finality of the ocean voyage to Europe I had taken with my parents, the widening space of dark, oily water between ship and dock that meant we were physically severed from New York, the exciting sense of remoteness that days of seeing nothing but ocean can give.

The plane trip was uneventful except for the first glimmer of lights along the coast of France. It was night when we landed, and Miss Waldron had arranged for us to stay at the Hilton at Orly. It did seem impractical to try to get into Paris at two in the morning, I suppose, and Maria was not in the least interested in Paris. France to her was Egan. She had grudgingly consented to driving down to Belan-les-hauts and taking two days for the trip, which could have been done a lot more leisurely if not for her impatience, but her eagerness to see Egan was more understandable to me than my wish to immerse myself into the countryside was to her. I agreed that I would be satisfied to leave Paris for the end of the summer when maybe Egan might accompany us for a few days, and so that night I resigned myself to the comfort of a good bed and an American-style bathroom.

The little car we had rented was parked outside the hotel the next morning. We were shown how to shift gears, and then with our luggage in the trunk and strewn over the back seat, I got behind the wheel and turned the car south.

It didn't matter to me that Maria slept most of the time, or followed me indifferently into dark cool churches, and along the narrow sidewalks of narrow old streets. "Quaint," was her word. "It's really quaint, Carrie," she said, mustering up the semblance of enthusiasm so as not to quench my pleasure. As if she could. We stayed on the back roads; we stopped at walled towns, and at turreted châteaux; we followed wide green rivers meandering through stone town embankments and through sunbaked meadows. We spent the night in an enchanting place called Sarlat, where our stuffy bedrooms and lumpy pillows were compensated by the cobbled square outside, the shops behind the arcades, the trailing geraniums brightening the stone walls, the sweep of cliffs beyond. I wished I could stay to paint the magnificent profusion of flowers massed in copper basins wherever we turned. "Quaint," said Maria. "How did you ever find this place?"

By the next afternoon we had reached the mountains. The driving was slow, but the vistas were breathtaking. Shifting gears on the constantly corkscrewing roads tired me more than I expected, and we made frequent stops, slowing us up. Once, toward evening, we stopped at a sandy clearing near a village plaza and watched sunburned men roll heavy metal balls, like bowling. The air was cooler, and smelled of fruit and wine and garlic; the mountains towered, stony and rust colored in the setting sun.

"It's getting late, Carrie," she said.

I knew it was late, but I didn't dare suggest spending another night en route. I don't think she could have stood it.

"Everyone will be asleep by the time we get there," she grumbled.

"Not Egan. He'll certainly wait up for you," I said, shifting into second as we began a downward spiral.

"He won't expect me anymore. He'll never think we're driving in the mountains at night."

I thought it was crazy myself. I hadn't expected the scenery to be so wild. There were only the flimsiest of guardrails to mark the precipices on one side of the road, and it was impossible to increase our speed. To make the going even rougher, it began to rain.

Maria was growing grumpy. "We could have flown down to Nice and rented a car there."

"And miss all this?"

I had to stop even now, to flex my numbed arms and stiff back. When I got out onto the road the blackness was overwhelming, the wet air perfumed with lavendar which grew on the softer slopes. I picked a sprig in the light of the headlamps, and crushed it between my fingers. I picked a second sprig to hand Maria.

"Lavender," I said. "Imagine, in these mountains."

"Maybe I ought to drive," she said. "At least we'd get there."

But I was afraid we wouldn't, with Maria driving, not impatient as she was, not on these roads. I had only one fear and that was that the car would break down, because if it did we would be helpless. It had been at least an hour since we had passed another car.

I tried to distract her. "Can you imagine yourself spending your life as mistress of a country hotel?"

"I might, if I had to," she said sulkily, refusing to be distracted.

It was a foolish question. What limits were there to their life together, with the Waldron money? I tried again. "Is the older brother married?"

"He was. He's divorced. If you hadn't wasted so much time you could have had a detailed autobiography from him. *If* he'd talk to you, and there are times when he doesn't."

"I *am* sorry, Maria. I didn't really expect we'd take this long. I had no idea what kind of a road it was. But I'd looked forward so much to the drive—"

"Don't feel sorry, Carrie, I'm a selfish monster," she said at once, sitting up with a resigned sigh.

It was Maria who saw the sign first. I was too busy trying to make out the outlines of the road. "There!"

BELAN-LES-HAUTS, read the low white rectangle, 2.6 KMS.

"We made it," I said, more relieved than I wanted to admit. "And it's not even midnight."

"We're not there yet. And after, the worst part is the road from Belan to La Ferme." She hunched forward to see through the streaming windshield. "You have to go through the town, and then there's this little dirt road you have to watch for."

We were through Belan-les-hauts almost before we knew we had reached it. A few streetlamps bordering the plaza almost extinguished by the full, spreading trees, a light in the back of a shuttered café, and in a *boulangerie* where I suppose they were baking bread for the morning, and we were out into the streaming darkness again.

Maria's face was pressed to the glass. If I hadn't been crawling we might have passed the small sign, LA FERME, and an arrow, and, awkwardly lettered, HÔTEL PITTORESQUE. VUE***.

At least it had pretensions to picturesqueness. And a view. I backed to make the turn, and found myself facing a river of mud.

"They could have thrown down some gravel," I muttered.

"They have. It washes away. They're going to tar it as soon as they get some money."

We were beginning to spiral around another mountain, literally, on that slippery ooze. If I'd have had more sense, or if I'd known how long we still had to travel, I would have turned back to Belan and stayed in the car until morning. This time there weren't even guardrails, only the glistening shrubs to tell us the road ended and a precipice lay below it. My head was beginning to ache with the effort to see; I don't know how many spirals we had made, when I glimpsed high above a lamp hanging over a gate.

"That must be it," I began, when suddenly I was blinded by two powerful headlights coming straight at us. Maria screamed. I blew the horn loudly, squeezing as far to the side as I could. Maria gave another faint scream. Almost on top of us, the car swerved, and tore down the mountainside, hidden by the curve before we could turn and see it.

For a few minutes I didn't try to move. I just fought for breath. "Maniac," I said. "He couldn't help but see us. He might have stopped to see if we were all right."

Her face looked small and pale. "It's as if he wanted to force us off the road."

"Nonsense," I said. "Who'd expect another car at this time of night? He must have been drunk."

I made myself start up the motor again, and we drove up and up until we passed through an iron gate, one side rusting and fallen and overgrown by vines. We were in an open courtyard. I wasn't going to leave the car here, the porch was still too far away, and the rain showed no sign of letting up. I drove to the porch and parked in front of the steps and fell back against the seat, too exhausted to move. I was vaguely aware of an ungainly stone structure, with a round turret at one end roofed in peaked red tiles like the roofs of Provence, tall trees surrounding us buffeted furiously by the wind. The lantern in the porch was swaying dangerously.

But Maria was now wide awake, her fright forgotten, already pulling on her raincoat and jamming a rain hat flat on her hair. She was out of the car and running up the steps, pressing her finger to the bell. I could hear it pealing twice, three times.

A light appeared in the turret, and minutes later lights appeared in the second floor, and then on the first floor. The door opened and an old woman peered out, sparse gray hair in two braids, a flannel robe knotted around her, the high ruffles of a nightdress covering her neck.

"What do you want at this time of night?" she said, in French.

"Mlle. Sophie, don't you remember me? I'm Maria Waldron."

The old woman's unyielding expression did not change, but she opened the door wide enough for Maria to come in. Maria waved to me. I made a run for it through the rain up the porch steps.

"My friend, Miss Belding."

Mlle. Sophie's glance was sharp. "We did not expect you anymore tonight," she said. "It is no time for arrivals, and departures, and quarrels— One has to get up and work in the morning. No consideration at all, not even to lower their voices—"

We were in a cavernous stone hall of what was more like a manor house than a farmhouse. The stairs were wide and made of stone, uncarpeted, and except for the tall, lecternlike desk with the ledger open on it and a board with keys behind it there was no sign that we were in a hotel. La Ferme was cold and unwelcoming, and we had been nearly killed coming here. I shivered.

"Fill out the forms, please," said Mlle. Sophie, gesturing at the cards on the lectern.

Was she going to insist on all that now, couldn't it wait till morning? It couldn't. Mlle. Sophie folded her arms while Maria and I filled out the cards.

"Your passports."

Resignedly I dug into my damp handbag to produce mine. Maria made a face at me, her eyes saying, I'll tell you about her later.

"I will show you to your rooms," Mlle. Sophie said, drawing the flannel robe tightly about her as she moved toward the drafty stairs.

A door slammed above, and there were running feet. A young man peered down at us from the balustrade, and for an instant he looked as if he might leap over it. Instead he took the last flight of stairs two at a time and made for Maria. They were pressed in each other's arms.

I am not scientific-minded, which is why I suppose that I tend to trust first impressions. He is in love with her. It is very plain. Wordless, they held each other as if they couldn't get enough of each other. I felt like crying, maybe because I was so glad for Maria.

"One goes, another comes," said Mlle. Sophie with disdain.

It drew them a little apart.

"Why didn't you phone?"

"I'll never learn to use your phone system if I live a thousand years. Besides, aren't they on strike?"

"It is awful, I know. Why didn't you plan to get here during daylight? If I'd known you were on the road on a night like this—"

"And someone tried to kill us. Someone coming from La Ferme—"

A stillness fell. "What?" he said.

"Ask Carrie."

He suddenly found time to notice me.

"Carrie," he said contritely, putting out his hand. "Welcome to La Ferme. I'm sorry it's been such a damp welcome." But his mind was plainly elsewhere. "What's Maria talking about?"

"Maria is being dramatic," I said. "Some idiot of a driver came right at us on that stretch of road just below the gate. He must have been drunk, because he would have had to see our headlights."

"Did you see what kind of car it was?"

"We were both blinded by his lights." I paused. "But he must have been here at the hotel. Didn't you hear him?"

"He might have been lost, and mistaken our road for the throughway." He gestured at his robe and pajamas. "Anyway, I was in bed. I gave up on Maria's coming around midnight—"

"It was all Carrie's fault," Maria broke in. "She made us stop and admire every ruin, every sprig of lavender."

"Ugly American," he said, and pulled off her yellow rainhat.

"If you will permit me, I will go to my room," said Mlle.

Sophie. "Decent people sleep at night, so they are fit to do their work in the morning."

She swept past me in that faded cotton flannel robe; I glanced up then and met her eyes. They were full of hate. I was taken aback. Cold mounted from the stone floor clear through me. She's senile. Or mad. Or both.

"Mlle. Sophie is worse than last year," Maria whispered.

He cuffed her cheek, as if he needed a pretext to touch her. "Pay no attention to cousin Sophie," he said. "Actually, she's quite cracked."

He smiled at me, and irresistibly I smiled back. The dim light from the cobweb-wreathed chandelier dotted with moths shone down on his dark head. He was like so many young Frenchmen one sees dashing about in their open sports cars, wearing turtlenecks and jeans, their faces reflecting a kind of recklessness and carelessness that is so very attractive if it does not inconvenience you. Lean, browned by the sun, his cheekbones high, his nose straight and his eyes gray and fine, he would have just been another extraordinarily handsome young man if it were not for the look on his face, tender, amused, as if there were nothing he did not understand or would not accept in this life.

"Your luggage," he said. "Let me get it for you."

"You'll get wet. Take my raincoat," Maria said, putting it around him.

"You can reach the trunk from the steps," I called after him. "I parked the car right beside them. I hope it's okay."

The moment he was outside Maria turned to me. "Well?" she demanded, her eyes shining.

"Would you mind if I fell in love with him, too?"

"*Terribly,*" she said, laughing.

He came back with our valises, and hung her raincoat over the stair rail.

"Are you cold? Hungry?" he said. "There's cheese and fruit. And brandy. And tea."

"All I want is to get into bed," I said.

"Well, I'm not sleepy at all," Maria said, and no doubt she wasn't, after having napped for most of the two-day trip to Belan. "Are you sleepy, Egan?"

"Not anymore," he said, and grinned at me.

"I'd like some fruit, and lots of talk," she said. "I'll wait for you down here, Egan, until you take Carrie to her room. Where's Conor?"

"Sleeping. He's been putting in a backbreaking day on the new pool."

"You did put in a pool!" she cried. "Oh, great!"

"Conor's desperate to lure the tourists here. We can't offer them the river to bathe in; it's too shallow and it has a rocky bottom. He's done most of the work himself."

"It's the least he can do."

"You're heartless, Maria. But let me take you upstairs, Carrie."

I followed him up those chill steps and down a dark corridor lined with doors. Opening one, he showed me into a large room with high ceilings and whitewashed walls streaked with damp; there was a curtained washbasin alcove with a bidet that one had to fill from a tin pitcher, and a wide sloping bed covered with a faded quilt. Why don't country hotels at least put in brighter bulbs? I thought resignedly. It was no worse than I had expected, and I would buy a new bulb when I went to Belan.

"The bathroom is across the hall, and Maria will be in the

room next to yours. I hope you don't mind not having a private bathroom. That's a luxury we'll have in time, I hope."

It was a luxury I rarely could afford, when I traveled. "I don't mind in the least. I'll be very comfortable here."

"Maria said you were nice." Again that tender smile.

I looked away, and my eyes happened to catch the bottoms of his pajama legs. They were pale blue, as were his leather slippers, and the spots of dried mud stood out plainly on them.

"Sure you don't want something warm? To help you sleep?"

I forced my eyes away. "Thanks, but I don't need any help in sleeping tonight!"

"Then, *bonne nuit.*"

"*Bonne nuit.*"

At least there was hot water, due no doubt to the older brother who was the engineer and good with the plumbing. I washed at the washbasin with a tiny piece of soap and dried with a towel that had been darned in several places. I did not bother to draw the drapes; they looked so dusty I thought it best to leave them undisturbed, and anyway, there was nothing outside the window but a black, looming mountain. I did turn back the quilt to inspect the bed, which I do only when the bed is questionable, and this one was. The sheets, though coarse and mended, were clean.

I turned out the light and pushed open the long casement windows. The wind rushed in with a scent of wet pine and a gust of rain, and I hurried into bed and pulled up the quilt. The bed rolled and spun like the road we had come on, and then gradually righted itself.

Mlle. Sophie's baleful eyes haunted me. I thought of her

disjointed talk, a quarrel, raised voices, someone leaving—
Had someone left the hotel just before our arrival, and did
Egan know of it? Why should he want to conceal it? Those
spots on his pajamas—he must have been outside in them.
And yet he had been so emphatic about knowing nothing.

In the silence of my room I heard the exquisite sound of
soughing branches, heavy with rain. Next to the crash and
surge of surf breaking, this is my favorite sound. I was on a
mountaintop in France, and ahead of me lay a long, beautiful
summer. I forgot everything, the cold unwelcoming hotel,
Mlle. Sophie's eyes, even the car that had tried to drive us off
the road, in my total pleasure.

2

I awoke to the same soughing sound, but with a difference.
There was a new crispness to it. The rain had stopped, and
there was a line of pearly mist moving up the mountainside.
The room looked less dingy in this dappled light. The furnishings were locally made. I'm sure, but handsome. There
was a large carved armoire facing my bed, and rush-seated
chairs. The floor was the red-tiled floor of the South.

But when I put my feet down, the mat beside the bed was
soiled, as was the doily under the lamp beside the bed. Mlle.
Sophie was undoubtedly too old to be housekeeper anymore,
if she had ever been adequate. I dressed, and went out to
Maria's room and tapped lightly on her door. I did not mean
to disturb her if she was sleeping, and who knew when she
had finally gone to bed. She murmured something about seeing me later and I went on downstairs myself.

There were dead flies and moths in the corners of the steps, and a smell of insect spray. I am by no means a conscientious housekeeper, I'm too easily distracted, and when I stay at the most rustic inn I'll forgive disorder if there is charm, but at La Ferme there was neither charm nor cleanliness. When I looked through glass doors into the dining room the white cloths on some of the tables were stained with wine and coffee, and littered with crumbs which had spilled onto the shabby carpet beneath. Someone would undoubtedly ready the dining room for the next meal, but the departing guest would take an unpleasant impression with him. Maybe there was more New England tidiness in me than I imagined, maybe my mother's prim, immaculate house was more ingrained than I wanted it to be, but I had a wild impulse to whisk away the soiled cloths and run the vacuum.

I pushed open the glass doors from the musty salon and found myself outside on a graveled terrace through which weeds were poking up. There were several round metal tables rusting on it, along with equally rusting chairs. Breakfast had been served there this morning; there were still heavy cream-colored pottery coffeepots on two of the tables, and baskets with a slice of bread left in them—not even the morning *croissants?* I wondered, but then it was probably too early for them—and the telltale spots of jam on the cloths. Even as I stood there a small car with luggage laced precariously under a tarpaulin on its roof backed up noisily in the cleared space behind the house and moved gingerly down the road.

When the motor died away the silence was again complete. No, a distant hammering, the ring of stone. A small sign had been lettered and stuck in the ground, with an arrow pointing: PISCINE. The way to the swimming pool. I followed the gravel path under the trees and came out onto a clearing below the house. Turquoise water gleamed like a shining eye in the oval of slate and concrete. A man knelt at the far end, fitting in stones and tapping them with a hammer. He wore only a pair of faded dungarees, and a brush of fair hair shone silvery in the sun. This must be Conor.

He didn't hear me approach in my sneakered feet, not until I was within a few feet of him.

"Good morning." I spoke first.

He gave me a long look. It was almost surprised. I am not that unconventional looking. Perhaps he thought that Maria's companion would be older, and more comfortable in her appearance, or maybe even stern and suspicious, behind silver-rimmed glasses. Companions in my mind always seem to fall into one group or the other, and are rarely under thirty. I had pulled my hair back and fastened it with a rubber band, and without makeup I look younger than I am.

"You're Miss Belding?" There was a definite question in it, so I was right, and I was not the way he had imagined me.

"Carrie," I said. "And you're Conor."

We were both wordless. I too had to substitute a new image for him, I too was disconcerted. I had thought of him as an older Egan, heavier, more dissolute, with perhaps a thin black mustache as befits a man who would heedlessly gamble away another man's inheritance. He was heavier than Egan, a big man, taller too, fair skin burned brown—I could tell how fair from the line of skin where the dungarees began—and I could see now that the fair thatch of hair was laced with some gray, and there were lines in his forehead and about his eyes which showed pale in his tan.

I began hurriedly, aware that I had been staring, "It's a

lovely morning, after last night—" but he too had been searching for something to say, and had come up with at the same time:

"Breakfast is late. Egan just left for town for the bread. Unless you don't mind last night's, toasted over. I can fix you some coffee."

"I'll wait for Egan," I said.

"Egan overslept," he said. "I suppose you came very late."

"It was about one," I said. "I went to bed, and left Maria up with Egan, so I suppose they were up for hours later."

He bent his head over the piece of slate and using the hammer and a chisel cut away a triangle from one end.

I said, "You've made a beautiful pool."

"It hasn't paid off so far," he said briefly.

"Maybe you ought to advertise it," I said. "Your sign doesn't mention it."

He gave me a quick glance from under sun-bleached eyebrows. "I've been meaning to have a sign made. There just hasn't been any time. We're understaffed, as I'm sure you've already noticed."

"I'd imagine you'd have trouble getting help up here. It's so out of the way."

"It's not its being out of the way," he said. "There are women in the village who'd come up here. We haven't the cash to pay them." He was being more defensive than he had to be. "Maria must have told you this is a losing operation."

I said, "I suppose a new hotel needs time, before people find out about it, and tell other people."

His gray eyes glinted. "And what do you think they'll tell other people about La Ferme?" he said dryly.

He broke in while I was still trying to formulate an answer, "It's one of those circles again, see. We can't provide the amenities because there isn't enough business. And there isn't enough business because we can't provide the amenities."

I began, "You could borrow from a bank—"

"If you ran a bank, would you invest in La Ferme?"

"It's beautiful, the trees, the mountain, the air."

Again that quick glance. "I happen to agree with you. That makes two of us. Ask Egan if he'd choose to spend two months here. Or your friend Maria. Right now there isn't even a decent road. The traffic south takes the Route Nationale, which is good and fast."

"But—" I hesitated. "You did decide it had a chance as a hotel."

"That's because I have no business sense whatsoever," he said. "Because I worked on a conviction. One of these days there just won't be an inch of room left in these Riviera resorts. People are going to look for unspoiled places where there's air to breathe and space to walk and sun and cool nights, places that are relatively cheap. If we ever get a decent road, they'll find their way here."

He hammered in the slate he had trimmed, and stared at it. "And I could be wrong. I've been wrong before."

He must have known that Maria would tell me about his gambling away their money. His mouth tightened, and color came up into his face.

"I want only to see La Ferme on its feet, maybe showing a little profit. Then I'll hand it over to Egan. It'll be all his, and I'll clear out."

I said, "You mean, you could leave this place forever?"

He looked at me sharply to see if I was joking. When he

saw I wasn't, his expression changed. He said quietly, "I've always loved it here. I came summers, after my mother married Jarret and moved to France. You can't imagine how it looked to me after my grandparents' apartment in New York. I lived with them the rest of the year." He stopped, musing. He said, "I thought there couldn't be any spot more beautiful."

I thought of my own apartment in New York. I could understand.

"My mother was charmed with La Ferme from the start. That was why she put so much of her own money into it. My stepfather couldn't afford to keep it up and had let it fall into ruin. When they both died within a few years of each other, the estate went to seed again. Sophie just grubbed out a place to eat and sleep in. She's been housekeeper here as long as I can remember."

He stopped abruptly, as if he had allowed himself to say too much, and leaned over to find another piece of slate from the pile behind him. I stared at his sunburned back, at the hair glinting silver on his neck. I was aware of a prodigality in him that was more than physical dimension, more than ceaseless work and tireless drive. I thought of the way he had spoken of La Ferme. If he loved something, or someone, it would be complete, extravagant. And yet something else lay beneath the surface, something I sensed, but could not really grasp. His curtness, his aloofness were a protective cover to hide something he did not dare disclose— But I was allowing my imagination to romp on in a way I had; I checked myself. All I could be sure of was that he was a man on his guard.

A battered Citroën came to a stop beside the kitchen entrance almost hidden by trees. Egan got out, carrying a basket on each arm. From one, long loaves of bread protruded, from the other, those round green-and-white-striped melons that seem to grow only in France.

"You can get your breakfast now," Conor said, dismissing me.

I lingered, I don't know why.

"If you stay," he said almost grimly, "I'll probably ask you questions I'll regret. One doesn't look a gift horse in the mouth, and we can certainly use the income you're bringing in."

"What questions?"

"Like, why are you here? To see that Maria doesn't make a fool of herself over Egan?"

I hadn't expected such bluntness. I recovered. "Do you think I could prevent it?"

"Then why *are* you here?"

"Do you ask that of your other guests?"

To do him justice, he reddened. "They don't stay all summer. They spend the night and they're on their way."

"As it happens, I did expect to come here to France this summer, even without Maria. To paint."

He looked at me from under his brows. "You're an artist?"

"I'm trying."

He gave a short laugh. "That explains your kindness to La Ferme. Only an artist would see something in it."

I felt a curious need to be honest with him. "But Maria's aunt did ask me to keep an eye on her. She's very young. She might need some help with her own feelings."

"Someone who might spot a fortune hunter a hell of a lot quicker than Maria?"

"Wouldn't it be only fair to her that she should know, if he were?"

"Carrie!"

It was Maria, waving at me from beyond the pool. "Having breakfast?"

"Be right there."

I met his eyes full on. He said, "Have your breakfast. You shouldn't have come, but now you're here, it's too late, and she's involved, and there's nothing you can do about it."

He turned his back on me, terminating the conversation. I went slowly back to the terrace, badly shaken. He knew something that was profoundly troubling, and somehow we had become part of it. Had it only to do with Maria and Egan, or was I involved now, too? There was an ominousness to the way he had spoken that was hard to put out of my mind, in spite of the flawless morning.

The table in front of Maria was covered with little pots and pitchers, and a basket of *petit pains* and *croissants*. Their fragrance reminded me that I was hungry.

"So he actually talked to you," Maria said, pouring coffee. "You should feel flattered. Usually it's only yes or no with me."

I thought irrelevantly of the car that had tried to drive us off the road last night. Someone who was merely drunk, or careless, or someone who wanted to frighten us away? Conor? "Can you imagine any reason why Conor should not want us to stay?" I said. He had said himself that he could use the income we brought.

She shrugged. "Maybe he's a white slaver. And he's afraid we'll see too much."

"And Mlle. Sophie is the leader of the mob."

She giggled.

"Seriously, Maria. Did you feel last year that you weren't wanted here?"

She shook her head. "I was only here for two weeks. I hardly saw Conor."

"Maybe it's me they don't want."

She stared. "But why, Carrie?"

"I don't know." I took a *croissant* and passed her the basket. "Well, no matter what he thinks of me, I found him rather attractive."

Her eyes widened. "You did!"

I had to laugh, she was so astonished.

She said soberly, "He's too old for you. He's forty."

"I didn't notice."

Her expression was even more sober. "Before you start getting ideas, I think you should know he has a mistress."

I put some jam on my *croissant*. The jam slipped off the crisp crust, and I took pains to maneuver it back on again. I didn't want Maria to see that her words had inexplicably filled me with dismay. It was ridiculous. I had just met him. Suppose he did have a mistress?

I was grateful when Egan joined us at that moment, and she had eyes only for him. He stretched out his long legs in jeans, his feet in rope sandals, and appropriated Maria's cup to pour himself some coffee. It was as if he had performed something intimate; a little pulse throbbed in her throat. I didn't want Maria hurt. She was almost too guileless, too artless. I suppose growing up in that large house among servants, with only ailing, crotchety Miss Waldron to turn to, she was hungry for love. I was afraid for her, suddenly. She cared for Egan altogether too much.

"So you've met Conor," Egan said.

I nodded.

"You mustn't mind him if he's ungracious now and then.

Underneath that grim exterior beats a good heart. I'm not joking, really. Conor's a good sort. The best, actually."

Maria said, "Carrie thinks he's attractive."

He smiled. "Good for you, Carrie. He does manage to put off a lot of people."

"Not Laure," Maria said.

He flashed her a look of annoyance.

"I had to tell Carrie about Laure. She's going to meet her very soon, and she'll find out for herself."

"I did ask you not to talk about her," he chided her gently. "Conor wants it kept a secret, and so does she."

I changed the subject. "You and he are very different, Egan."

He grinned. "I'm somewhat more sociable? As a matter of fact, Conor's changed a lot. But then he's had some rotten luck."

"The money?"

"Other things." He hesitated. "Well, you might as well know. His marriage broke up before he came here. His wife had one of those glamor jobs in fashion, more important to her than anything, than a baby, than Conor even. Maybe his losing all that money was the last straw. She couldn't see herself living a life of hard work, so they split up. I don't think he expected it." He put down his coffee cup. "He's been driving himself ever since he came here as if demons were on his back."

"I suppose he wants very much to make up to you what he lost."

"I've told him I don't care. I've told him he doesn't owe me anything. I've told him I'll get along."

Maria watched him quietly.

He said, "The odd thing is, he's caught up in exactly what he tried to get away from. He thought the gamble in stocks would give him freedom. Now he's more tied down than before."

I said, "But he's answerable to no one here." Except his own conscience, which could be the most inexorable of masters.

"What's the difference? He's breaking his back for a few crummy dollars. I don't believe in that, not for a crummy few thousand."

Not for a crummy few thousand. Not when I could marry millions.

I glanced involuntarily at Maria. Had that thought occurred to her, too?

Her face was unclouded. She said, "You're both so ready to believe he's driving himself just for Egan. But when he lost all that money it wasn't for Egan. It was for himself. He wanted the freedom you're talking about for himself. If he didn't want it so badly he wouldn't have risked Egan's money, too."

Egan smiled. "Maria's a bit prejudiced. Not that I mind too much."

"I think he wants money so he can get Laure to marry him. Laure would never marry a poor man," Maria said. "Not the way she likes to live."

Egan rose. "You talk too much. Just for that, help me carry in the breakfast dishes."

She jumped up, only too pleased.

How would Egan get along, without Maria's money? I could imagine him drifting through life by Maria's side, handsome, agreeable, always charming. People who take responsibilities lightly are always charming company. To some it might appear a wasted life. Would Conor think so? Was that why we worried about their relationship? No, it was more than that. The tone of his voice when he talked had told me that.

I went up to my room. I remembered my promise to write Miss Waldron my first impressions. There was a writing tablet in my valise still unpacked; I found it, and sat down in front of the window.

"Dear Miss Waldron," I wrote, "I've only met Egan twice so far, and have had only the briefest of conversations with him, so it is hard to form any judgment. But I can see why Maria, or anyone else for that matter, could fall in love with him. He is not only attractive, but he is gentle and tender to her. I believe he is very much in love with her, too. Of course this is only a first impression, which is what you asked for . . ."

I stopped. Inexplicably I had a vision of Conor bending over those slates, his fair hair silvery in the sun. I tried to dismiss it and get on with the letter, but it was as if I were gripped in an emotion too strong for me. Shaken and confused, I stared at the words I had written. Who was I to write of love? Maybe it was easier to recognize in someone else.

III

1

MLLE. SOPHIE STALKED the corridors of La
Ferme. I told myself she would change when she grew ac-
customed to us and discovered we were harmless, but she
seemed to grow increasingly hostile. I wondered if she had
imagined we would find La Ferme so distasteful that we
would pack up and leave. I began to dread the smell of violet
talcum, that distinctive aroma of genteel ladies of the turn of
the century, that announced her presence. It was worse than
the insect spray the chambermaid Sylvie left behind in my
room each morning, which lingered no matter how speedily I
would fling open the windows to let in fresh air. I did not
give up attempting to win over Mlle. Sophie, but resolutely
smiled and said good morning or evening to her when we
passed, but she would only mutter something in response that
I did not understand. I could not fail to understand her dark
glance, however; it said, why do you stay where you are not
welcome?

I was sure she would soften toward Maria, who was even

more persistently and sunnily agreeable toward her. More than that, Maria insisted on doing many chores about the hotel to be with Egan. She carried glasses and china and silver to the dining room before meals; she folded napkins with the flourish of a professional; she stamped the small brown crocks of butter with the crest of the Jarrets. I think she would have even helped Egan at meals if he had not insisted that at those times at least she conduct herself like a guest.

But Mlle. Sophie was as unyieldingly hostile to Maria as she was to me. When I complained to Maria once that whenever I asked Sylvie for a fresh towel or another small cake of soap, my request was invariably transmitted to Mlle. Sophie, who brought it, towel or soap, to me herself as if she were bringing me some great gift I had been crude enough to demand. Maria said only, "Don't mind her, please, Carrie."

"I really don't. It's just that I wish I knew why. She was set against us from the start."

She looked down. "She's cracked, as Egan says. Now and then—" She hesitated, as if unwilling to tell me, and then she tried to laugh. "—Well, it's as if she were a child. I'll find a dead spider on my pillow case. I know it could have been squashed in the laundry or something, but— And sometimes when I open my door I find her standing there, as if she had been listening. I don't know what she could be listening for. Egan never stays very long when he does come in, which isn't often—" She took a breath. "I really don't care. She can't help herself. You mustn't mind either, Carrie."

Most of the time Maria was with Egan, so she could put Mlle. Sophie out of her thoughts. If she weren't helping him around the hotel she would be off in the little car we had rented, with Egan driving, to Belan to market, to Digne for the more important shopping, or to the movies. Sometimes they even drove to Nice or Cannes, and came home very late; on those nights she put up her hair and wore a long skirt, so I suppose they went dancing.

They invariably asked me to join them, and I invariably refused. I was not going to be pushed into the role of chaperone, which I had been promised was not my job. I didn't really mind being alone. I'd be out on the mountainside nearly all day painting, and by night I would be languid with sun and drunk with fresh air. If there were congenial guests on the terrace I would have a drink and some conversation with them. Otherwise I would sit in the salon, where Mlle. Sophie never came, and read. The fine furniture smelled of must, and moths would sail in through the open doors to spin madly around the crystal chandelier until they stunned themselves and fell to the needlepoint rug. The heap of little gray corpses would gradually increase until one day Sylvie would come with broom and dustpan and sweep them all up.

I think unconsciously I was waiting for Conor to come and speak to me, but he never did. He might have stopped in to greet me, as hotelkeeper to guest, but it was as if he were deliberately avoiding me. It was true that he was busy from early to late. No matter what hour I started out in the morning with my painting gear over my shoulder, my lunch of bread and cheese and fruit in a string bag, I could already hear the sound of his hammer or saw from the carpenter's shed. Or, when I climbed above La Ferme and looked down on it, I could see him moving about with a shovel or a spade, bare to the waist except when the mistral blew cold from the north. His silver-laced hair gleamed like fish scales in the sun.

I always mentioned how hard both the brothers worked in

my letters to Miss Waldron. It was the sort of detail I thought she would approve of, and it was true, besides. They might work differently, Conor as if he were hounded by Furies, Egan as if he must help Conor even if he were sure it was a lost cause; still, between them they kept La Ferme in operation.

I also wrote that Maria was happy. I wondered at first if she would soon tire of the chores that filled her day, if this might not be the means of disenchanting her of both La Ferme and Egan. But it seemed to be having the opposite effect. Maria must always have had friendships thrust on her without any effort on her part; it was as if Egan made himself more desirable by her having to work to be near him. No, I couldn't really believe it was only this. I had complete conviction that it was more than a schoolgirl amour with Maria, that she was genuinely in love.

When I wrote about Egan I made a point of not stressing his charm. "Charm" was a word that would set Miss Waldron's teeth on edge, that would cloud not only Maria's common sense but mine. There was more to Egan than charm; Maria felt it, too, I was sure. Under the ingratiating good looks lay something hard—determination or purpose?— and the assurance that he would succeed. The assurance may have come from women; working as he did behind the desks of luxury hotels, he must have always been a target for those wealthy, lonely women who come looking for excitement and love. But what was his intent? Was it only to marry a wealthy girl like Maria, or was it more than that? In his own way he was curiously like his brother. Something drove Egan as well, but he managed it more confidently, and it did not trouble him as it did Conor. But all this was a feeling so vague, so merely sensed, that I did not mention it in my letters to Miss

Waldron. I said he was purposeful, I said he was likable, and he was.

One morning on my way out I stopped Sylvie and asked her to replace the linen mat at my bed. I had spilled linseed oil on it the night before, from a carelessly capped bottle among my painting things.

"I'm not sure. Mlle. Sophie—" Sylvie looked unhappy.

Just a white linen mat, the kind most hotels change every day, to put your feet on when you step out of bed. I suppose I was insistent.

She glanced behind her. The cupboard door was open, but Mlle. Sophie was in another room and out of sight. Sylvie scurried to the cupboard and came back with a fresh mat, pushing the soiled one down to the bottom of her cart with the used towels. I went back to my room for my gear. When I came out, I found Mlle. Sophie with the stained mat in her hand. She turned on Sylvie, and poured out a torrent of French in a voice that hissed like a snake's.

I had to speak up. I said, "It was my fault, Mlle. Sophie. I insisted on the clean mat."

"How dare you insist in this house! You are an intruder!"

"I am a paying guest," I said quietly.

"Servants are not to be trusted with linen!"

Sylvie's face whitened in anger. "You call me a thief?"

"This house is cursed! With thieves and criminals—"

"If you must blame someone for the mat, blame me, not Sylvie," I said, even though I could tell she was too furious to hear me. The whole episode was outrageous, and Mlle. Sophie should be kept from having anything to do with the guests.

I didn't see Sylvie when I returned that evening, but then

there were no other guests and Egan served dinner, so I assumed she had gone home early. Egan and Maria left immediately after dinner, and I carried my glass out to the terrace where I sat until dark, making the brandy last. I had just decided to go up to my room when Conor came out. My heart gave a great leap; so we were to meet again at last.

But almost at once I could see he had something unpleasant to say. His words stunned me. "It might be better if you would let Sophie give the servants orders."

I finally found my voice. "Give the servants orders?"

"Sophie collared me. She was hysterical. She said you interfered with Sylvie, and now Sylvie's quit."

I was angry by now. "I only asked Sylvie for a clean mat, and she gave it to me. It was Mlle. Sophie who practically called her a thief."

He stared. "Hell." He turned on his heel and walked away, and then came back. "I should have known. It didn't seem like you."

I was too angry now even to answer.

His face was furrowed. "I'm sorry."

I was smarting, and not ready to forgive him. "It seems to me you might talk to Mlle. Sophie about the way she acts to your guests." I remembered my promise to Maria, and kept silent about Sophie harassing her. "She's more than unfriendly. She's hostile."

He drew in his breath. "She's getting irrational. Still, she does a job here."

"Do you think so?"

His eyebrows lifted. "What do you mean?"

I said to myself, well, he's an engineer and not a hotel-keeper by training, and he hasn't noticed Sophie's housekeeping. And then I thought of his desperate and futile efforts to make something of La Ferme, and of Mlle. Sophie destroying what he tried to do. Still, I might have kept quiet if her accusation hadn't rankled.

"I don't often stay at hotels even as grand as La Ferme," I said, "so it isn't as if I'm used to plush places. But I've noticed that whatever else is neglected, in a French hotel you can be pretty sure of the bed and the table. Not here."

He seemed bewildered. "Our food is damn good."

"It is. And Berthe is great. But the tablecloths! And all that cracked china. And the sheets falling apart. And everything looks as if it could stand a good scrubbing."

He seemed trying to take in my words. "I never thought . . . I guess I've just figured that things were getting older and there isn't any money to replace them." He looked at me. "You can't blame Sophie for that."

"Some things don't cost money," I said shortly. "Like running a vacuum."

"Sophie doesn't like the vacuum."

"But that's just the point! She doesn't seem to care what the hotel looks like, either! Or the tone she takes with guests—"

We were so absorbed we didn't hear Egan and Maria come up behind us.

"What are you two so serious about?" Egan said.

Conor made a brusque gesture. "Sylvie left us."

"Damn," said Egan. "And Laure is bringing friends with her."

So I was to see Laure at last!

"That's not till the day after tomorrow," Conor said. "Is there anyone in Belan who wants a job?"

"I'll ask around tomorrow," Egan said. He turned to Maria. "Coming up?"

She nodded. "Night, Carrie. Conor."

They went upstairs, their arms around each other.

Conor's face was still furrowed. I don't know what upset him more, his unjust criticism of me, or what I had said about the hotel. I was already conscience-stricken for having spoken out against Mlle. Sophie. She was old and disturbed, and not accountable for what she did. I should have over-looked her lie. Conor had more compassion than I. I liked him for it. If I hadn't liked him as much even before I might not have felt so sorry for him, for the losing battle he was fighting, for which she was partly responsible. If I hadn't felt so sorry for him I would have felt sorrier for her, for her age and senility and twisted mind.

I said, "It's hard to deal with people when they're as old as she is. Old people seem to magnify the things you say out of all proportion. I suppose they have so much more time to themselves to brood."

"Sophie never wanted La Ferme turned into a hotel," he said. "We couldn't seem to make her understand that it was the only way we could hang onto it. My stepfather would have lost it if he hadn't married my mother and she hadn't put her own money into it. Sophie felt we had disgraced the Jarrets by turning La Ferme into a business. The Jarrets were once important around here. She felt we had sullied the name." He gave a short laugh.

"What would she have done, if you'd abandoned La Ferme?"

"Lord only knows. But she has these delusions. Egan says she's cracked, which is putting it harshly. She doesn't even remember that my stepfather let her stay out of charity, for whatever work she did around the place. She wasn't even the housekeeper when they were here. My mother always brought a staff down from Paris. She was more the caretaker in their absence. But she imagines herself the mistress of La Ferme."

"Couldn't you tell her the work was too much for her?"

"Then she'd be living here on our charity, and she's too proud for that. She's living in past glories. And it once was quite an establishment," he said. "Maybe it was because I was younger, and more easily dazzled, but La Ferme seemed as grand and opulent to me then as a king's palace."

"What happened to it, that opulence you seem to remember?"

"I've often asked myself that," he said. "Maybe they sold everything along with the things in their apartment in Paris. Egan doesn't remember. He thinks they asked him if he wanted to keep anything, when the lawyers were settling up, but he said no. He was a kid in his teens. He didn't want the contents of a household."

He frowned, as if conjuring up an image. "I remember the way the terrace looked, when it was set for guests. Embroidered linen, silver candlesticks— I had a Persian rug in my room that I used to love, full of those tiny vines and flowers—" He caught himself. "I suppose I could check with the lawyers, but it won't bring anything back."

He shrugged. "Maybe I just dreamed it. It's gone, along with a lot of other things."

He left abruptly, barely remembering to say good night. He seemed overwhelmed by the enormity of what had happened, not just to La Ferme and its vanished splendor, but to himself. I supposed he meant his marriage when he talked of the lost good things. Or maybe he even meant that money on which he had counted for his freedom. And yet I had the strange feeling that it was something else, something that went even deeper.

It might be Laure.

I was bewildered to realize that his unhappiness was important to me. He's attractive, he's hurt—and he's the only other man here, I told myself flippantly, so of course I would be involved. It can't be anything more.

2

In the morning Egan brought Camille from the village to take Sylvie's place. She was a plain, solidly built girl with fiery cheeks, and carried a bulging suitcase tied with a strap; she was going to live at La Ferme, which Sylvie had refused to do because of the loneliness. Now Egan would be free of some of his tasks, which made Maria happy. When Egan saw me at breakfast he told me that Camille had worked at the café in Belan, and would be able to take care of La Ferme's bar in the evening, which often kept him from getting away as fast as he wanted.

That same day when I went up to my room to collect my fear I heard the unfamiliar sound of the vacuum. So Conor had weighed my criticism, and decided to speak to Mlle. Sophie. She would be furious at me, no doubt, but I had the feeling that Conor understood I only wanted to help, which was somehow very important to me. And as for Sophie, she was furious at me anyway, even when I did nothing.

I think if I hadn't felt that Conor realized that I wanted to help, I would never have had the courage to press Egan to buy the green cupboard for La Ferme.

Egan caught me, as they were leaving. "How about coming with us? Maria and I are taking a run over to a farm not far from here. The people are selling out and moving away, and Conor thought we might pick up a few tools he needs cheap."

It sounded interesting. I hesitated, again because I did not like to be an intruder on their outings.

Maria came down the steps. "Come on with us, Carrie!"

So I went.

The farmhouse was the same gray stone as La Ferme, but smaller and cruder, a working farm rather than a gentleman's estate. The courtyard smelled of chickens and ducks, and there were feathers in the beaten-down earth. Egan went to the barn to poke around, but the farmer's wife beckoned to us to come inside the house. Everything would be sold at auction on Saturday; she hoped we might pay a little more. The small room that served as sitting room, dining room and kitchen was colorful, the dark interior brightened with fresh flowers. Why couldn't Mlle. Sophie do as much for La Ferme? Flowers grew in profusion there.

The cupboard caught my eye at once. It seemed more Italian than French, a faded green with open shelves above and shelves behind doors below, painted gaily with scrolls and garlands. Instantly I thought of the bare, whitewashed entry hall at La Ferme, with no furnishings but the lectern, and a gloomy family portrait.

"Wouldn't this be pretty at the hotel?"

Maria paused, and looked at it doubtfully. I honestly don't believe she was aware of her surroundings at La Ferme; they were simply an unimportant backdrop for Egan.

"You mean, Egan should buy it? I'll ask him."

Egan came in, led by Maria. He looked at it, and laughed at us both.

"Conor would hit the ceiling if I wasted any money on furniture."

"It wouldn't be wasted, Egan. It would be so important for the hotel to look more . . . inviting."

The farmer's wife was anxious to sell, and dropped the price twice when Egan continued to shake his head. Finally I said, "If Conor doesn't want it, I'll buy it from you and ship it home when I leave."

So we brought it back to La Ferme, lashed to the roof of the Citroën and swathed in an old quilt. As inducement the farmer's wife had thrown in some thick faïence plates like those made around Strasbourg, with rose flowers and pierced rims. I carried them carefully on my lap as we drove very slowly home. All I could think of was how pleased Conor would be at the transformation. And I was sure it would be a transformation. I would take one of those copper kettles that hung on the kitchen wall, no longer used, and fill it with flowers to stand on the chest, with the Strasbourg plates to line the open shelves above it.

Camille came out to help us carry the cupboard inside. She polished the copper kettle while I went outside and picked an armful of gladioli and poppies and other flowers whose names I didn't even know.

When I was finished I was amazed myself at the change. The whitewashed walls and dark wood seemed to take on a glow they never had before. The entry seemed to promise beauties elsewhere in the hotel, which was what I had expected of it. Even Egan lifted his eyebrows. He went out to look for Conor.

Mlle. Sophie must have been somewhere about all the time we were hauling and pushing the cupboard into place; she must have heard the sounds we made, and our voices. But suddenly she appeared at the head of the stairs, words spilling from her in a fury as she descended.

"And who is to dust this monstrosity?" she spat. "Who will bring fresh flowers? Does one of you fine ladies plan to spend her leisure in housework?"

Maria and I were too dumbfounded to answer.

Egan and Conor came in then.

Mlle. Sophie turned on them. "You allowed them to bring this into your father's house, this piece of crudeness from some farmer's hut?"

Even Egan was stunned for the moment by her assault. Conor stared uncomfortably over our heads. Egan recovered quickly, and went to Sophie and put his arms around her.

"Sophie dear, you don't recognize an antique when you see one. And hand-painted, too. Our guests will go wild over it, you'll see, and one day we'll sell it at a large profit!"

She brushed his arms away angrily.

"You have brought disgrace on this house in many ways, Egan, you and your brother both! You bring in that foul money which corrupts you, your evil business! The only mercy is that there is none of your father's line left to see the consequences!"

Conor's voice was unexpectedly sharp. "That's enough, Sophie."

She whirled on him. "It is your doing!"

Her black-clad figure darted to the stairs with amazing agility, as if hate had infused her with energy. We could only stare after her dumbly.

Maria broke the silence, her voice as reedlike and plaintive as a frightened child's. "What does she mean, Egan? Does she mean me?"

Conor turned on his heel and walked out.

"No, of course not, Maria! I told you not to pay any attention to her." He took her around. "She's been going on like this for years. It's because she hasn't forgiven Conor for turning La Ferme into a hotel. Or me for allowing it."

"But what she said . . . foul money—"

"That's what she calls the money we make by running the hotel. She's always muttering about how low we've sunk. And she doesn't remember what she says half the time. You have to promise me not to listen to her."

I went outside, leaving Egan to console her. I wished I could see Conor. All my good intentions to help him had ended in this ugly confrontation. Foul money. Did she really mean what the hotel brought in, or had she actually been referring to Maria's money? Did she and Conor both know something about Maria? Or was it something else, something so disturbing that Conor had left without a word, that Egan was less than convincing in his attempts to reassure Maria?

I did not feel like painting anymore. I did not want to stay at La Ferme either and meet Mlle. Sophie again, so I went for a long walk. I climbed so high that I left the leafy trees behind and even the pines and firs were beginning to thin out. I walked on a slippery carpet of green moss through which the stone skeleton of the mountain emerged. Was Sophie the reason for Conor's troubled state of mind?

I came up with no answers, and only a deeper preoccupation with the disturbing atmosphere of La Ferme. It was late when I got back to the hotel, and went up toward my room. I passed Maria's door, and tapped on it to see if she was in.

She was. She had just bathed, and was dressed for dancing, in a long striped skirt with a wide belt clasped around her waist. If she had been upset by the cupboard incident she now showed no signs of it. Egan must have been very effective in smoothing away all the unpleasantness, because she was radiant.

She said, "Isn't Mlle. Sophie something? I suppose every old house should have a character like that, to give it a spooky feeling."

They were going to drive to Cannes, to a discothèque Egan knew, she said, slipping bangles on her wrists.

"Egan is coming to New York in September, he told me," she said. "He even said he might stay with us, if Aunt Millie invited him, and I'll see that she does. She probably would love it, actually. She's so anxious to see what he's like."

"Is he coming just to visit?"

"He might even look for a job at a New York hotel. This way we won't be separated for a whole winter. He doesn't want to be separated from me, either."

At least then they would do nothing final this summer. I knew I couldn't have stopped her if that was what she wanted, and yet there was something here at La Ferme that made me uneasy, and I would not want her involved until I knew.

I said casually, "What is this Laure like?"

She wasn't fooled by my manner; her eyes shone.

"You are interested, aren't you?"

I shrugged. "She's coming tomorrow. I'll find out soon enough by myself."

"It's just so funny, to think of you being that curious. Do

you want to know if she's pretty?" She stuck out her lip judiciously. "Not pretty. Sort of gorgeous, in a lush way. Maybe she was pretty when she was young. She's old now, like Conor. I'd say at least thirty-five."

"Why doesn't she come here more often, if she's his mistress?"

"She can't, she—"

She stopped.

"I promised Egan I wouldn't discuss her," she said.

"Don't then. I'll assume she's married."

Her mouth fell open. "How did you— Now, I didn't tell you, did I?"

"No, you didn't. Where is her husband?"

"I *can't*, Carrie."

And she didn't, even though she might have during dinner. At least it explained why Laure came so seldom, and implied a reason for Conor's frustration.

Camille was proving so efficient that Egan was able to leave immediately after dinner with Maria. Camille brought trays of coffee to the few guests sitting out on the terrace, her cheeks even more fiery, and little wisps of hair stuck to her forehead, but without other signs of tiring.

But I hadn't shaken off the ugliness of that afternoon as easily as Maria, perhaps because I had no Egan to distract me. I could not bring myself even to fall into conversation with the other guests, and went into the salon where I would be alone, and tried to read. I did not expect to see Conor. The pattern had been fairly well established, and so I was left momentarily speechless when he turned up there. Our eyes met for a long instant, equally troubled.

He said awkwardly, "I like the cupboard. I realize now

how much the place needs touches like that. I'm glad you thought of it. Thanks."

His hesitancy gave me the courage to speak honestly. "I'm sorry I ever thought of it. I didn't mean to bring on what happened today. I never dreamed she would react as she did."

"Sophie? Forget about her."

"You mean, she was just talking out of thin air?"

He looked at me a long minute. "Do you have any reason to think she wasn't?"

"It's none of my business," I said. "You can say it if you want. But there's Maria, and Egan, and so . . . I can't help but think about it."

"You'd be wiser to forget what she said. She rambles."

"Then there's nothing to it?"

He didn't answer at once. Then he said, "The one thing that made sense was that I was responsible for what's happened. She's right enough there."

"About the hotel?"

He gestured. "About . . . everything." He added wryly, "I'm sure Maria must have told it all to you."

"You mean about your losing that money your mother left?"

"I didn't lose it. I gambled it," he said. "And like all gamblers, I was convinced I was on to something sure."

"You must have had good reason."

"I know something about minerals. It was a branch of engineering I hoped to go into, but I was convinced it wasn't as practical as construction. My grandparents wanted me to be practical, unlike my mother who married a penniless Frenchman and spent my father's money to maintain him."

He said, "I don't usually go in for this kind of breast-beating."

I ignored that. "What did you invest in?"

"Know anything about sulfur?"

I shook my head.

"It's in short supply. The method of extracting it is expensive. The process I put our money into would have shortened the method of mining it. It seemed foolproof to me. It still does, and someday, somebody's going to make a fortune from it. But it needed more time and capital than we could raise. When the banks wouldn't put up any more, I even threw in Egan's share, but by then it was a lost cause. We went bankrupt."

"People make that kind of mistake. They don't blame themselves forever for it."

"It wasn't only the money," he said, "Egan left school. Not for lack of money. I was working, and could still have paid for his education. It went deeper. I influenced him in the kind of man he's become. He wants to copy me."

"Copy you?" I said. "Work the way you do?"

He ignored the irony. "I always wanted to be free of a nine-to-five existence. I hated every job I had. I wanted to get away to foreign places, work at the things that interested me. He was a kid, and impressionable. What the hell was he preparing to do with his own life, but slave at a desk and wait for the weekends?"

"You did prepare yourself for a profession first."

"And where did it land me? I couldn't even hold onto the money that was left for us. And now what was there but back to the grind, for both of us—"

He stopped. He must have seen on my face that he was

merely giving evidence to a supposition, reinforcing it with facts. Maria was the key to Egan's freedom just as that gamble with their money had been the key to Conor's. He said, "It isn't what you think."

I turned away. He would want to protect Egan; he felt he had damaged him enough as it was.

He said doggedly, "He's not after her money. You have to believe that."

I said, "The first day we met you told me you were sorry we had come. You hinted it was too bad that Maria was involved with Egan. Why?"

"I wasn't thinking of her money."

"Then *why?*"

He stared at me, his eyes sore as if he were cornered. "She's a kid. She'll need a hell of a lot more growing up before she can cope with . . . with a man like Egan."

"Don't you think loving him will help her cope?"

"No, I don't," he said turning on me. "It's not that romantic. I thought my wife loved me. When the chips were down, love had nothing to do with her choice. Maybe it made her hesitate a week or so longer than she might have if she hadn't loved me, but she chose her own life. Love helps you live with a problem, it doesn't help you solve it."

"What problems will Maria have with Egan?"

He tightened his mouth, and did not answer.

I persisted, "You mean because La Ferme is unsuccessful? What will that mean if he marries Maria? She can put enough money into it to transform it, or they can walk away from it forever."

He was still silent.

"Is it because you think he doesn't really care for her, that he's only using her?" I said it with a great deal of effort. I was afraid to hear his answer. I knew I would believe it, whatever it was.

He said, "He loves Maria."

I felt a swelling in my throat, I was so grateful. I said, "Then why shouldn't they have their chance together? Do you think it won't last? Do you think he's too sophisticated for her?"

He said, "I think she's the kind of girl he thought he'd lost forever."

Was he thinking of all those women, too?

"Why, aren't you glad for him then!"

He made a rough gesture. "It won't work."

"You keep hinting, but you don't say anything!"

"I can't say anything. I don't know anything. I'm only guessing, on the basis of . . . nothing concrete. She'd be better off if they'd never met." He hesitated, and then he said grimly, "And so would he."

He turned, as if he were afraid himself of the enormity of his implication.

"But, Conor—"

His troubled eyes rested on me. "Will you keep what I said to yourself?"

"If you want me to, but—" I was not being unfaithful to Maria. I would not change her feelings by relating more vague suppositions. Besides, what right had I to trust Conor so implicitly? Because I found him attractive? Might he not have his own reasons for casting doubts on their relationship?

He said, "I appreciate your wanting to help. I don't know why you should."

I could have told him why, if I had been ready to admit it to myself.

3

My curiosity to see Laure was so great that I think I would have stayed at La Ferme that day and given up my painting just so I would be on hand when she arrived. I was ashamed of myself; it was so immature, so . . . undignified. And I did not want to admit yet that Conor and the woman he loved should loom so large in my thoughts. So I made myself collect my painting gear and start out.

Camille was readying two rooms. Egan paused when he saw me staring into them.

"For Laure? And her friends?"

He nodded. "She always has the same room."

I said, "The cushions on the chair are frayed."

He laughed. "Laure won't care."

"But— If she's a regular visitor, shouldn't you see to it that she gets a fresh quilt, at least? Or maybe some flowers on the table?"

"Carrie darling, nothing could keep Laure away. Not the cushions, not the quilt."

He went off still laughing, and I got my lunch from Berthe and left. I walked to the vantage point I had found the previous day and set up my easel and squeezed paint on my palette and painted determinedly for some hours, not allowing myself to think. I wiped my hands and sat down on the grass and ate my lunch, staring at the succession of blue peaks that went one behind the other to the unseen Mediterranean.

I am in love with him.

I think I must have known it from the first moment when he looked up from the pool that morning and met my eyes, but I had to deny the knowledge to myself. It had happened too quickly to be reasonable, and after all, I was twenty-eight, not seventeen. And then there was Laure, which made it hopeless. But even if he had been free, there was the atmosphere of La Ferme, furtive, secret, hinting rather than overt, which should have made me want to turn my back on it and its owners.

Conor was not the kind of man I expected to love. I had imagined that man to strike like a whirlwind, shaking me savagely, sweeping me along with him by the force of his will. Who else could alter the course of my life? Large, untidy, remote, dogged, silent, bitter—a dozen adjectives came to mind, none of which should have made Conor appealing to me. Except of course that I did not think of him in those terms. I imagined him as a lover, warm, encompassing, as prodigal of himself in love as he was in his work.

Laure would know that side of him. Laure.

I made myself put paint on my canvas until the sun changed color and it was near evening, and only then did I pack up my things and start down the mountain.

I saw the car from above, curling up the road, and its long, ivory-colored hood made it different from the small, baggage-laden cars that usually found their way to the gates of La Ferme. I cut through the trees, and came into the courtyard only moments after it had come to a halt in the clearing.

I saw Maria at a table on the terrace, and I dropped into the empty chair beside her. Egan had gone to the parking area for their luggage. He opened the door for them. Now they were coming toward the terrace, Laure first, a man and woman trailing her, then Egan with the suitcases.

Conor appeared at the salon door, transformed by a jacket over his jeans, suddenly distinguished. My heart cramped with jealousy that he had done this for her.

"Conor darling," Laure said distinctly, and leaned forward

to proffer him her cheek. It was sociable and impersonal, and yet it was not. He kissed her, reddening.

Maria whispered, "For someone who has to be discreet, she doesn't have to *ask* him to kiss her."

Egan was steering them toward us.

"Maria, you know Laure, of course."

Laure was tall and smooth; a mane of blond hair fell over her shoulders, tangled by the wind. She was in sandals, and her toenails were pink. But it was her eyes that held me; they were as transparent and expressionless as water. She said, "It is the little American of last year. Yes, of course." She put out her hand. Her voice was rich and bland.

"And this is Carrie Belding," Egan said. "Mme. Patrelcis. Or Laure, as she insists we call her."

"How do you do?"

Perhaps I had been wrong about the eyes. They flicked over me without interest, not expressionless, only pale.

"And this is M. and Mme. Abdykian. Maria Waldron. Carrie Belding."

I noted that Mme. Abdykian was short and shapeless, with flat wings of graying black hair. When she held out her hand to me I saw two large diamonds on two fingers. Her husband, medium sized but with shoulders bulking under the shiny silk of his jacket, bent and kissed first Maria's hand, then mine. As he straightened up, I stared into his face, white, with eyes of polished black stone, unwinking. It was his mouth that smiled, and his voice was gay. "Why did you not tell us there would be such adorable guests, Laure?"

I was being imaginative. I was ready to see that coldness in Laure, that evil on M. Abdykian's pale face. Even if it had not been there I might have felt it, because of Laure—

"I must have a swim in your new pool before dinner. Show me what you have done with it since last week, Conor."

Laure put her arm through Conor's, and they went off together. She was not as tall, beside him, as I had first thought, but she walked beautifully, clinging a little.

"Such a dramatic setting," said Mme. Abdykian breathlessly. "It reminds me of our little inn above Corinth, is that not so, Armad? The air is so pure. No wonder Laure must come here."

"At least we know the reason for this dreadful drive," said Armad. His skin was that oily white that never tans, and under his close shave I could see the black follicles of his beard. Gold dazzled in his cuffs, in the cigarette case which he held out to Maria and me, in the lighter he whipped out for his cigarette. His shirt, his suit, his tie, even his shoes, were exquisitely made, the colors blending just so. His smile was constant, his glance admiring—and yet the chill had settled between my shoulder blades, the way it did when I kept my back to the mountain but could tell to the moment when the sun left its face and the first puff of wind blew from its shadow.

"May I bring you a drink?" Egan said to Mme. Abdykian. She looked at her husband, as if for permission.

"We will have two scotches in our room, please," he said. "We do not have Laure's vitality, which is inexhaustible."

"It is because she loves La Ferme so much, Armad," said Mme. Abdykian. "She says she is restored, revived, here."

The glance he gave her bordered on the contemptuous. He rose to go, and she scuttled after him. Egan followed with their luggage, turning around before he disappeared to make a wry face at us.

Maria laughed, and then, her face sobering, she said, "You sure you're all right, Carrie? You look sort of pale."

"I feel cold," I said. "Maybe I had too much sun today."

"They're funny, the Abdykians. I mean, you wouldn't imagine Laure having that kind of friends."

"They've never come here before?"

She shook her head. "Egan says they haven't. Egan says he once bumped into Armad by accident, in Cannes. Armad was with Laure and her husband, and he seemed sort of amusing, but Egan didn't think they were that close that she would bring them."

"I'm not sure I like him," I said, and shivered.

"Have you got a chill, Carrie?" she said. "Maybe you should have a hot bath."

"I'll be all right," I said. "I'll just go up and change."

But even as I went through the cold stone corridor it seemed to me that the atmosphere of La Ferme, which up to now had been a matter of an old woman's rambling, an accidental scrape on the road, Conor's warning words, had now solidified. It had grown oppressive, and actual.

Maria said, as we separated, "You don't like her either."

"I don't know her," I said.

"She *hates* me," said Maria. "I think it's because I'm young. Aging women feel threatened by young women."

I managed to laugh, somehow.

Maria and I had almost finished our dinner before Laure came down, followed by the Abdykians. Against the Abdykians, both of them in black, she moved like a goddess, small breasted and heavy limbed, her blond hair swept to the top of her head, pale-green chiffon floating behind her. Her costume was incongruous for La Ferme's dining room, and not only I, but the French couple who dined at the other table, stared. They could not know that Laure was dressing not for the audience of a provincial dining room but for Conor.

"Egan told me before he's sure she's forty," whispered Maria to me. "As old as Conor. She told us once she was married when she was fifteen, and her husband gave her that perfectly vulgar clip for their twenty-fifth wedding anniversary."

It was obscurely comforting that she was older than the thirty-five I had thought her to be. I was ashamed of myself for being so petty.

Maria kept watching Laure from under her lashes as if to discover signs of decay. From where we sat, the lifted line of Laure's chin, that betraying line, was flawless.

Egan served them himself, boning their fish at the serving table beside them, heating it over the flame, presenting it to them with a flourish, and a swirl of sauce. Laure laughed, and bowed her head to him as if acknowledging that it was an act, and a good one.

We were staring too long. I finally made Maria leave the dining room with me, and we went out to the terrace where Camille served us our coffee. Maria continuously looked at her watch, but Laure and the Abdykians stayed at dinner, keeping Egan in attendance. At last they appeared on the terrace, and Egan pulled over a table so that we might all sit together.

Laure said to me, "Conor tells me you are an artist."

I nodded.

"Indeed!" said M. Abdykian, drawing his chair so close to

mine that his cologne smothered the fresh evening air.

Laure said, "It would have to be an artist to place the cupboard there where you did. Conor is so completely unaware of the need for such decor. Those flowers are just what that ghastly lobby needed. I must say thank you for myself as well as for him."

I know I was wrong to resent her words for being so proprietary. Why should they not be? I muttered something about being glad she liked it.

"And if I find the lobby ghastly," said Laure, "I suppose you must find it even more so, as an artist."

"I've gotten used to it," I said. "Besides, I'm outdoors a great deal of the time."

"Ah, yes, Conor told me that you paint every day on the mountain," she said.

"May we see your paintings?" Armad said, politely.

"Of course, Carrie!" Egan said at once. "You must show them to Armad. Armad is a patron of the arts, isn't that so, Armad?"

Armad made a deprecating gesture.

"Laure's told us you are," Egan said, his eyes glinting. "It isn't often that we have guests here who can not only appreciate art, but afford it."

In a panic, I stammered, "I've only finished two, and I'm not sure—"

"Don't be modest, Carrie. I've seen them and they're excellent," Egan said.

"No, really—"

"You mustn't be shy—"

Laure broke in, her voice heavy with boredom, "Is it that important, Egan?"

It was her tone more than anything else, that suggestion that the paintings couldn't possibly be that interesting to anyone, that made me reverse myself. Let Armad see them; he might be as uncomfortable as I was, trying to come up with a reason not to buy them. I had left the canvasses drying on the bureau in my room, and I rose to get them. Egan stopped me.

"I'll get them, Carrie."

Our bedroom doors were never locked. He went inside, to return shortly with a canvas in each hand. But it had grown too dark to see, and he and M. Abdykian went into the salon with the paintings.

I pretended a nonchalance I did not feel. Maybe when I grow more professional I will feel so much inner confidence that I will be indifferent to others' opinions. But my work seemed so much a revelation of myself that I felt exposed, and I was not comfortable being exposed to the eyes of an Armad Abdykian.

I could see them in the salon, huddled over the paintings. At least Armad was paying them the compliment of giving them serious attention. They were quite good, I thought. One of them was of La Ferme itself, before I had ventured farther away; the tiled roofs and massed flowers made fine splashes of color. The other was starker, of the mountains and sky.

"I shall look at them, too," said Laure, rising in a cloud of chiffon and narcissus perfume. Now the three of them were staring at the canvasses.

Maria said, "You're not annoyed at Egan for suggesting it, are you? Because he does want to be helpful. He told me he was going to get Armad to buy one."

"He might have asked me first."

"You *are* annoyed," she said. "I told Egan you might be. But he said you were probably too modest to offer them for sale, but you had to get used to it, artists have to sell to live, and Armad is very rich."

They were coming back to the terrace now. Egan was smiling. "Not a bad start for a beginning agent, Carrie. We've made a sale."

"You are most accomplished," Armad said, giving me a little bow. "They are both charming, though I think Maria has chosen the better."

Maria? Startled, I looked at Maria, but she seemed equally surprised, although she managed to cover up almost at once.

Egan said smoothly, "You said you wanted to send the one of La Ferme to your guardian, isn't that so, Maria?"

"Oh, yes," she said. "To Aunt Millie."

"Maria wants her to see where she is spending the summer," Egan said. "Three hundred was the price, right, Carrie?"

"Right," I mumbled. I was certainly not going to take any money for the painting from Maria, if she wanted to send it to Miss Waldron, though I think the idea never occurred to her until this moment. It was probably enough for Maria that Egan had made the suggestion for her to go alone wholeheartedly, and without question.

Laure said, "You are quite talented, *chérie*. When Conor said you were an artist I was sure you would be only an enthusiastic amateur. Even in the galleries today the work seems no better than that of enthusiastic amateurs."

I found myself bridling at her praise. There seemed to be

in her an indifference to anything outside herself that made her words sound false and empty. There are beautiful women who are completely unself-conscious about their beauty; it is as if it were a fact long since accepted and could now be forgotten. But with Laure one felt it was a preoccupation. Maybe it was for the reason Maria had hinted; she was forty, and being beautiful now was a perilous state, constantly threatened. And especially if one wanted to be beautiful for a lover. She touched her hair, she studied her foot, she arranged a fold of her dress; when she looked at us it was not so much to see us as to see what we saw in her.

"Three hundred," said Armad. "Francs, or dollars?"

"Oh, Armad, dollars, of course," said Mme. Abdykian.

"We will give it to your niece as a wedding gift," he said to her. "Even though I had not planned on spending as much."

"We had thought to buy Murano glass," confided Mme. Abdykian. "But there is always the danger of breakage, shipping glass to America."

"Murano glass can't be compared to an original work of art," said Egan. "Haven't you someone you need to buy a fine gift for, Laure? Carrie will paint many more, I'm sure."

"One would think Carrie was paying you a commission," said Laure coolly.

There was a pause. "Brandy, Egan," Armad cried. "One always seals a transaction with brandy."

"Should you, Armad?" said Mme. Abdykian. "You've had so much already."

He did not even answer, turning in his chair so that his back was toward her.

Egan returned with a bottle and glasses for all of us. Only Mme. Abdykian refused. As if to challenge her, Armad filled

his glass twice. Conor came out, and Laure moved her chair
to make room for him beside her. A cold moon appeared, and
cast a bluish light.

Mme. Abdykian murmured about bedtime.

"Go to bed yourself," said Armad.

There was a silence. Mme. Abdykian opened and shut her
mouth, and then rose.

"Forgive me, but I am tired," she said. "Good night."

"You are not tired, Anna, you are old," Armad called after
her.

"You are insufferable," Laure said, with disgust.

"But why go to bed with Anna," said Armad, "when there
is all this youth and beauty here?"

"I'm taking one youthful beauty away for a walk," said
Egan. He held out his hand to Maria, and she jumped up.

Laure's eyes followed them, her mouth suddenly hard. She
hates me because I am young, Maria had said. I could see that
Maria might be right. I couldn't blame her for being envi-
ous; she and Conor were compelled to sit side by side, not
touching, or even talking to each other more than necessary.
All they had was the night, when everyone else slept.

Armad put his hand on my arm.

"Egan says you are spending the summer here. To keep an
eye on our little heiress, yes?"

"Armad, you are being unusually disagreeable, even for
you," said Laure, without raising her voice.

"But Laure dearest, why should a young woman come to
this ruin of a place?" said Armad. "I mean no disrespect for
your efforts, Conor, you understand. Maria's reasons are
obvious. Egan is irresistible to women, but for a desirable
woman like Carrie to immure herself here for the summer

without male companionship—" He shrugged. His voice had thickened. When he reached out for the brandy bottle his hand wove helplessly, searching for it.

"Shouldn't you go to bed?" Laure said.

"We have hardly begun to get acquainted," said Armad, leaning forward to put his damp palm on my knee.

I shifted my knee, but Conor had risen instantly.

"Let me help you to your room, Armad," he said, grasping Armad by the elbow.

"But I am not at all sleepy," mumbled Armad. Conor propelled his sagging feet toward the French doors. They vanished inside.

Laure studied me. "You mustn't be offended by Armad," she said. "Though he *is* offensive. I dislike him especially when he drinks."

My unspoken question was: Then why do you choose to travel with him? She answered it almost as if she had heard it.

"He is my husband's cousin, and a member of Sarif's firm. When he invited himself to accompany me I could scarcely refuse, especially in my husband's presence."

I said, "But why should he want to come here?"

She touched her throat, she studied her jeweled fingers. "Perhaps he is curious about my . . . my retreat, as my husband calls it. It is a year now that I have been coming here. My husband always makes jokes about it, my retreat. I only come of course when Sarif returns to Istanbul. When he is in Cannes, there are always guests. I have a great need to be alone."

She preferred to maintain this fiction even with me then, although she must have guessed Maria would tell me what Egan told her. Unless Egan was not supposed to tell Maria.

He had shown annoyance when Maria had mentioned Laure to me.

"How did you discover La Ferme?" I asked her.

"Through Egan. He worked at St. Moritz two years ago. He uses people very gracefully. He asked me to tell my friends about this hotel his brother was operating, and when I came myself to see it, I . . . I found it suited my needs."

"It needs a great many things to make it attractive," I said. "But it could be done."

"With money," she said indifferently. "I have offered Conor money, as an investment even, not a gift, but he will not take it. He is a difficult man. Don't you find him so? Inflexible, dour. But attractive. Yes?"

She stared at me.

She can't be jealous of me, too, even if I am younger, I thought. I felt like a wren beside all that splendidly formed, creamy flesh. "Yes," I said quietly. "Very attractive."

Conor was returning. He stopped at my chair. "I'm sorry about Armad."

"It was all right."

"He passed out cold before I got him into his bed."

"How Anna stands him," murmured Laure.

He said, uncomfortably, "I'm going up to bed myself. I'm up early, and—"

"There is no need to explain, darling," said Laure. "We understand."

"Egan will lock up when he comes back."

We waited until he had gone, and then I said, "I'm going up, too."

I did not want to cause her any embarrassment about following him. Or perhaps she would not have found it embarrassing.

"I'll come with you. It's so dark here at night." She shuddered delicately, and we went in together.

At the head of the stairs we said good night, and parted. She came after me.

"I would lock my door if I were you," she said. "Armad might wake. I am French, you know, and I still find the men of my new country strange. They are strict with their wives and daughters, and guard them jealously, in a quite medieval way. But foreign women are different. They imagine there are no limits to your freedom."

I thanked her, and locked my door. I wasn't sleepy yet. I waited for Laure to finish with the bathroom so I could go in. I heard the door open, and her moving toward her room; when I opened my door I saw her in her white peignoir turn not to her room but toward the tower stairs where Conor's room was.

I did not want her to know I had seen her going to Conor, and I waited for a few moments until she disappeared up the circular steps before I ventured out across the hall to the bathroom. The floor was still flooded from someone's bath, and on the white tub a long black hair was stuck, Mme. Abdykian's. I shuddered, and spread out a towel on the floor so my slippers would not get wet.

Cautiously this time I opened the bathroom door only a crack before I came out. No one was in sight, and so I went back to my room. But before I closed my door I heard another door open. It was Armad. I thought of Laure's words—could he be coming to my room?—and for a moment I stood transfixed. But, no. Armad was making his careful, noiseless way toward the turret steps. I waited, but he did not come down.

4

I didn't sleep well that night. I listened to the sounds of the trees through my open window, but the sound did not lift me up as it had that first night. It had a mournful undertone that cramped my heart, that reminded me of the end of summer when I would go back to my tidy loft and my tidy life at Misses Burns. And when I did sleep, I woke once with a start, imagining I saw Armad bending over my bed. I was glad when it was morning. I did not want to see him or Laure, and I dressed quickly and took my painting gear downstairs with me. I ate a peach at the kitchen table, and a stale roll, and then with another peach in the string bag and a wedge of Brie I went out into the fresh-smelling air that already gave promise of heat.

Just in front of me, on my path, stood Conor, almost as if he had been waiting for me.

"You're up early," he said.

"So are you."

I had imagined him to be sleeping later than usual, after Laure had come to him. Maybe he guessed my thoughts, because color came up into his face.

"I can't stay in bed these mornings. Besides, I like to work before anyone else is up. I seem to be able to think more clearly." There were furrows in his forehead.

He should have looked happier, or at least more relaxed, after his night with Laure. I was irritated with myself for the way my thoughts kept dwelling on it, imagining their bodies pressed together, her long hair tangled on his shoulders. Was that why he looked so troubled now, knowing she would be gone by lunchtime?

"Off for the day?" he said awkwardly, as if casting about for something to say.

"It's too far to walk, if I try to make it back by lunch," I said. "And the light changes so fast."

He said, "I'm sorry about Abdykian last night."

"It wasn't anything. But he is unpleasant."

"I . . . never met him before. I didn't know who Laure was bringing with her."

"I suppose you'd have to take him in, in any case, when you run a hotel."

"He . . . didn't bother you last night any more?"

"I locked my door. Laure told me to."

He shifted his feet. "I heard him in the hall, I thought. Well. As long as he didn't bother you. Don't let me keep you from this light."

I continued up the mountain. Forget about Conor. You came here to paint, not to find a lover. At least you knew about Laure before it could go too far.

Only it had gone further than I wanted it to. I'd always been so sure it would be instant recognition when I met the man I could love; that he would be someone who loved someone else had never figured in my concept. The best recourse for me now would be to pack up and get away fast, only I was tied to Maria, not only because of Miss Waldron, but by my own conscience. I couldn't abandon her now.

I filled the canvas with brilliant slashes of color, determined to shut him out of my mind. Let Egan sell as many paintings as he could; I didn't want to take any souvenirs back to New York with me of La Ferme, and I might at least have some money in my pocket for my summer.

The sun faded, the air turned chilly, I packed up and

started back. When I reached the gate I found Maria waiting
for me.

"How nice," I said, putting my free arm through hers.

"I've been worrying about you."

"About me?"

"You just seemed so disturbed, yesterday."

"Oh. That was Armad, that's all."

"He is awful. But in a way he's funny."

I hadn't thought him funny. I had thought him dangerous.
I must be too emotionally snarled in all of them, I was losing
my sense of humor. So, suppose he had put his hand on my
knee? Unwelcome hands had found their way to me before.
Suppose his eyes were without a trace of humanity, of
warmth or love or pity— Could I be projecting my own feelings about Laure? But he had been spying on Conor and
Laure last night, of that I was sure. Idle curiosity? Prurience?
A Peeping Tom?

"Anyway, they've gone now," she said. "I almost feel sorry
for Conor. She's the only pleasure he has, and he has so little
of that."

"Hmm," I said.

"And she's really mad about him. Egan says she's even
suspicious of you and me, staying here. He says there was
never any other man in her life but her husband, until she
met Conor, that her husband is very jealous of her and she's
afraid of him, but she loves Conor so much she's even taking
that chance."

I said, "I suppose there's a deep dark reason for your telling me all this,"

"Look," she said, "you're my teacher, and a few years older
and all, and I'm not supposed to be very bright—"

"I never said that. Or even thought it."

"Well, I'm sure it's what my Aunt Millie told you about me. And maybe I was different before I met Egan. I think he's changed me a lot."

Miss Waldron might even be alarmed to hear that.

"Anyway, I think I know enough about being in love now to worry about you."

"Who said I was in love?"

"You don't have to say it. I can see the difference in you."

"You just never saw me away from school before," I said, trying still to make light of it. "Naturally I'm different when I'm on my vacation—"

"Don't talk about it if you don't want to," she said. "I just wish it weren't Conor."

People were sitting on the terrace having their aperitifs. Egan, passing with a tray, smiled at Maria. She blew him a kiss as we crossed into the salon and mounted the stairs to our rooms. It seemed to me that the corridor still smelled of narcissus.

Conor did not appear at dinner. Camille brought us our food, the white earthenware tureen with delicious steaming soup, the simple but excellent lamb. If people would only find out about La Ferme, if Mlle. Sophie would only polish it up, present it fresh and bedecked with flowers like the countryside around it—

Would it really matter to anyone? One day Laure would brave her husband and demand a divorce, and then, loaded with money and jewels she would come for Conor, and he would shake the dust of La Ferme from his heels forever.

Egan and Maria disappeared after dinner. I finished my

coffee alone. I talked to a young Belgian couple who had accidentally stumbled on La Ferme and who did not seem unhappy about their shabby accommodations.

"It is a discovery, this place, so high in the mountains," said the girl. "Now that we know there's a pool, we shall tell all our friends who drive south to stop here."

Something must be done to advertise the pool. I was still wide awake when they went to bed, and walked down to the shed that Conor used as his carpentry shop.

My hand fumbled in the dark until I found the light switch. The light illuminated a tidily organized work area. If only Conor could put his talent to the interior of La Ferme as efficiently! Lumber of all sizes was stacked according to dimension against the walls, paints were mounted on shelves, brushes hung below. I searched until I found a board that was just the right shape for a sign. There was sandpaper in a drawer; I sanded the wood until it was smooth, and then with a pencil I sketched in the outlines of La Ferme, surrounded by trees, with a series of mountain peaks as a background. In front, and prominently, I sketched in the oval pool. Conor's paints were for the house, quick-drying enamels, but they suited my purpose perfectly. I filled in the colors, unsubtle, bright, even naïve, but the effect was gay, and then I lettered in the name, LA FERME, and below it, PISCINE—POOL, to take care of both nationalities. A sprinkling of stars beside the name, after all, Michelin did not own the right to stars, and—

"Oh."

I don't know how long Conor was standing in the doorway.

"I saw the light on, and thought I'd forgotten to turn it off," he said. He came closer, and stared at the sign. "Say, that's very good."

"I didn't have anything to do," I said, shrugging it off. "And you did say you wanted a sign."

"I didn't expect you to go to that much trouble. And it's a lot prettier than the man in Belan could do."

Our conversation was exhausted. I said, "Well, I'll go up to my room and get some turpentine for my hands."

"I've got some here." He found the bottle and a clean rag, and stood watching me while I cleaned the paint from under my nails. "I'll see you back to the hotel," he said, when I'd finished. "I have a flashlight."

He turned out the shed lights behind us, and took my arm, the other holding a dancing beam of light on the uneven ground.

"It must be pretty lonely for you at night," he said. "I know it's a job, but still, it's too bad that you have to be stuck in a place like this."

"I honestly don't mind," I said. "I'm used to being alone."

"If you're alone," he said slowly, "it must be your own choice."

I flushed a little, because Conor was not the kind of man who sprinkled his conversation with bits of social flattery. "I don't meet that many people," I said. "And of the ones I do, there aren't that many that I want to . . . to know better."

"Having someone you care for makes a hell of a difference," he said. "Nothing matters, where you are, what you do, if you're with someone you care about."

"You have Laure," I said.

For a moment he didn't answer. Then he said, "Laure is married."

"It's you she seems to love."

He flung out his arms in a gesture of futility. I suppose he was thinking of the brief hours they had together. Still, it was better than nothing.

"Why doesn't she divorce her husband?" I said.

"He'll never give her a divorce. He'll never let her go."

"Can he keep her, if she wants to leave him? I'm sure she'd be willing to ask for nothing—"

"Must we talk about Laure?" he said, turning on me.

"I'm sorry. I didn't mean—"

He clamped his mouth tight. "You don't know anything about her . . . us."

"And it's none of my business. I understand."

"No, you don't. You don't understand a damn thing," he said with unexpected anger. "And I don't want to talk about it."

I tried to speak calmly. "There's no reason why you should."

"I don't know why Laure had to come up. I only wanted to thank you, again."

"For the sign? You don't have to. It was a labor of love."

I thought to dismiss it lightly; instead I called it precisely what it was. I said good night in a hurry before I would disclose something else I preferred to keep to myself. I went upstairs.

Maria's door was open. I glanced in; I hadn't seen her return with Egan, and I thought I would say good night. She wasn't alone. Egan and she faced each other.

I felt the tension. Had they quarreled? I retreated. "I only wanted—"

I stopped. In the dim light I hadn't noticed their faces before. Egan's was a mask, Maria's was white.

"What's the matter?" I said sharply.

They looked at each other as if they couldn't decide whether to speak or not. It was Maria who blurted out: "Look."

She held open the door of the armoire.

I hesitated, suddenly afraid. My thoughts conjured up a dozen terrible things I might see. But I went forward and peered into the armoire. At first I saw only a tangle of rags. It was moments before I realized that the rags were Maria's dresses. Someone had slashed at them with a razor.

I caught my breath. Only torn dresses. But my skin crawled. It was as if the slashes had been directed at Maria's flesh.

"Oh," I said faintly. "Your pretty dresses. I—" My words fell away. I put my arm around her and held her as if I could stave off any harm.

"It's all right, Carrie," she said, trying to control her own voice. "It's only a few dresses. I'll get some more. I shouldn't have told you. I was afraid you'd be upset."

Over her head I met Egan's eyes.

He said in a strained voice, "It must have been Sophie. I'll speak to her." He made a move to go, but Maria broke away from me.

"Egan! Please."

He waited.

She said, "It won't make any difference. She's crazy. But I'm not afraid of her, honestly. Don't make any more trouble for her."

Again Egan and I exchanged looks.

"Maybe Maria's right," I said. "Sophie may even be more enraged if you interfere. The dresses aren't important. Maria is."

He turned back to Maria. "I'll drive you into Cannes tomorrow, and I'll buy you the most beautiful dresses we can find."

"As if I cared about the darn dresses," she said shakily. But she was smiling, at least.

I left them. For the first time I wondered about Maria's safety. The next day I had even more occasion to wonder. But not to wonder, only. To be truly afraid for her.

In the morning it rained, and Egan and Maria decided to put off their trip to Cannes. I stayed in my room, painting what I could see from my window, the flaking stone walls, the weedy terrace, the rusting garden furniture, the flower heads drenched in rain and hanging low. My door was open, so Camille could come in and tidy the room.

Egan looked in. "Hard at work? Is it all right to interrupt?"

"Come in." I continued to work, and he watched over my shoulder.

"Carrie, are you worried about Maria?"

"Shouldn't I be?"

"I won't let any harm come to Maria," he said. "You can be sure of that."

"You may not always be able to prevent it."

"Sophie won't hurt her. She may try crazy tricks like yesterday's, but she won't touch Maria."

"How can you be so sure?"

"I know her. She'll scheme and hatch out things like those dresses, all in her head. But she'd stop short of anything serious. Do you think I'd let Maria stay on if I thought she was in danger?"

I looked at him. I don't think he would have, but he was more concerned than he was letting on. "Suppose it's someone else? Not Sophie at all?"

His face stiffened into the mask it had been last night. "Who else could it be?"

"I don't know." I looked at him evenly. "You would be more likely to know who would want to hurt her than I."

He said thinly, "I don't know of anyone. It's just some ghastly trick of Sophie's, that's all."

"I wish I could believe that."

"Don't worry about her, Carrie. I promise you as long as I'm here she'll be perfectly safe."

What could I say?

"Look," he said, with a visible effort to restore things to normal, "Maria is coming into Belan with me. How about driving with us? Armad asked me to take care of framing his painting. There's an excellent carpenter in the village. He made a lot of furniture for my mother, and I asked him to make up some frames for us. Maria can have one for the painting she's sending to her aunt, if she likes it. I thought you might approve of them before we crate them and ship them off."

I was ready to wipe the incident of last night from my mind, so I put away my paints. Maria was waiting for us in the kitchen vestibule where the raincoats hung; Conor's bright-yellow slicker was gone, so he must be working outside in spite of the downpour. Egan took his trench coat, and we ran to the car.

It was necessary to drive with nerve-racking care. The road was the same river of mud we had come here on, and in daylight it was even more frightening to see the steep chasm on one side. Perhaps as a reaction to our mood the previous night, our spirits unaccountably rose. We were able to laugh wildly when the car skidded, as if it were no more dangerous than a roller coaster, and somehow we made it into Belan without incident. While Egan parked Maria ran across the street to admire the elaborate little cakes in the *boulangerie*, and Egan bought us each one, which we ate hurrying through the rain to the carpenter's shop.

There was the familiar sour smell of raw wood and sawdust, the familiar excruciating whine of an electric saw. The old man himself brought the frames for us to see. They were massive, with hand-carved moldings. Only the touches of gold leaf had still to be put on. I picked one up, and was surprised by its lightness.

"Cheaper to ship," Egan said. "Like them?"

"They're very handsome. And they'll make the paintings look a lot more important than they really are."

"Armad was very impressed, I could tell, even though he tried to hide it. Thought I'd jack the price up if he let on," Egan said, grinning.

I ordered two more exactly the same; all my canvasses were the same size, so they would fit.

"It's all right, sending Armad's painting to your house?" Egan said to Maria as we left.

"Of course. You know I don't mind." Maria turned to me. "Once Egan sent a lovely blue velvet jewelry box from Florence to a friend who wanted to surprise his wife with it. He opened it when he came to pick it up and showed it to me, and I admired it so much he wrote Egan and Egan sent me one just like it."

"I don't like to be a nuisance," Egan said. "But you know

Armad. He might use his niece still honeymooning in Mexico as a reason to postpone buying the painting, so I told him you probably wouldn't mind."

The rain had stopped by the time we reached La Ferme. We were all feeling happier, and had managed to relegate the slashed dresses to some remote part of our minds.

Maria took advantage of the fact that no guests had arrived yet to take a leisurely soak in the bathtub. I saw her wander in with a jar of bath salts, a big cake of perfumed soap that we each had bought to supplement the tiny slab that was all Mlle. Sophie allowed us, and a box of bath powder.

"Sure you're not in a hurry for the tub?"

"I'll wait until before dinner."

I went back to my canvas. The mountainside would still be too drenched to walk there comfortably; I had become interested in the composition I had started before we went for the frames. I don't know how long I painted before I heard the scream.

It was Maria.

For a terrible second I couldn't move. Then I dropped my brushes and ran to my door. Egan was running from the kitchen. He reached the bathroom door moments after I began turning the door handle frantically.

"Maria!"

She opened the door herself, her bath towel held around her. The front of the towel was dyed red with blood.

"I'm okay," she whispered. "It's just my hand."

I seized another towel to cover her, and we took her back to her room. Egan caught her hand by the wrist. Her palm was deeply slashed. He bound her hand tightly in a linen towel hanging beside her washstand, while I went to the pharmacopoeia Miss Waldron's doctor had packed for us and found disinfectant and a gauze bandage.

Some color had come back into her face by the time we finished the bandage. I found her robe and helped her into it, and wrapped a towel around her wet hair.

"I don't know what happened," she said. "I was just soaking and enjoying myself, and then I started to soap myself up when I felt something cut me. It didn't even hurt very much. I guess I screamed when I saw all that blood—"

I left Egan with her, and went back to the bathroom. The tub was pink with her blood. Swallowing hard, overcoming a desire to be sick, I put my hand under the water, not knowing what I would come up with. My hand encountered her soap. Fortunately I nudged it first, and felt something sharp, and so I was warned. Picking it up gingerly, I stared at it. Barely visible, only a hairline showing, the edge of a razor showed buried in the fat pink cake.

Something moved just beyond my range of vision, something black. A smell of sickly sweet violets— I turned. Mlle. Sophie stood in the doorway, staring at the bathtub, at the bright drops of blood scattered across the mat. Her eyes narrowed, and she was gone, scurrying down the hall with that astonishing agility she could show when she wanted.

I ran into the hall. "Mlle. Sophie!"

Egan came out, in time to see her vanish up the turret stairs. He started for her when I called him back and showed him the soap in my hand.

"This is all we'll take from her," he said quietly. "She'll have to leave."

He went after her.

Conor came up the stairs. "What happened?"

I told him as objectively as I could. I showed him the soap. I told him about Maria's ruined dresses. Maria came to the doorway as I spoke.

"I'm all right, Carrie," she said. "Please don't make a fuss."

I think she was partly afraid we would decide it was best that she leave, but I think, too, that she could not bear to have Sophie hurt, even now.

"Where's Egan?" Conor said abruptly.

"He went after Sophie."

Conor started for the turret. Maria caught my arm. "Go with him, Carrie. They mustn't send Sophie away."

"If she's dangerous—"

"She'll die if she has to leave here. I won't have them send her away because of me."

I hesitated. But I wanted to respect her wishes; her pretty but still-wan face was all at once very grown-up. I ran after Conor.

Mlle. Sophie stood in her room, leaning against the wall as if she had been pushed as far as she could go. Her head was shaking so violently that her thin gray hair had come loose.

Her eyes found me as if I were her accuser.

"It was not I," she said in a harsh whisper. "There is a murderer in this house, but it is not I who did this." She glanced at Conor and Egan, and her voice rose. "They dare to accuse their cousin of such an act, I, who have always worked hard and feared God and served them even as children! They dare to accuse an innocent old woman of such an act!"

She swayed. I caught her. Her bones were like a bird's under my hands.

"No one knows who did it, Mlle. Sophie," I said. "No one knows for sure."

Egan helped me support her. We got her to her bed, and helped her lie down.

Conor said, "It's all right, Sophie. Maria is all right. Why don't you have a little nap before dinner?"

We left her. Suppose it were not Sophie? I looked from Conor's face to Egan's. They were shaken, but whether because of what happened, or because of the question of Sophie's guilt or innocence, I could not tell. Perhaps I am too trustful. I believed her when she said she was innocent, even though I could not imagine anyone else who could have done it.

Should I write Miss Waldron? I thought about it for several days, and then decided against it. Maria would not go home even if her aunt demanded that she do so. I felt sure of that. And it might only precipitate a drastic move by Maria and Egan. Better to say nothing and wait. And watch.

IV

$\sim$

$\sim$

$\sim$

1

MLLE. SOPHIE NEVER SEEMED to be the same after that day. She grew frailer and more faded, and the whalebone stiffness was gone from her back. On Tuesday Egan drove her to her physician at Nice. I remember the day because it was the day Foreign Junkets came. Maria went along to buy some things for her depleted wardrobe. Her manner to Sophie was as determinedly pleasant as always.

Someone was needed to stay behind and oversee the hotel, and I offered my services. Egan was grateful, Mlle. Sophie sullen. In her neat black coat and white gloves, she unlocked the linen cupboard and put out the necessary linen on Camille's cart and locked it again pointedly.

That morning I learned from Egan that Sophie had suffered a stroke some years back. If it had affected her mind, how could we hold her responsible for anything she did? *If* she was guilty. But who else? Of course it could have been any of the guests, and that included Laure and the Abdykians who had time before they left to insert the blade in Maria's soap. But for what possible reason, unless they were mad?

I found myself alone with nothing to do. I picked flowers, in such profusion that there were no containers to hold them all. I remembered the old and crazed china pieces; I might put some flowers in the dining room. The dining room could use the color; it would brighten those cloths.

Berthe said but, yes, when I asked if I might look in the pantry where the china was kept, and I found a number of sugar bowls without lids, pitchers that did not match anything. Berthe only shrugged when I asked if I could use them; no one had wanted them in years. I filled as many as I could with flowers, and put them out on each of the dining tables, reserving the long-stemmed ones for a big cracked soup tureen to put out on the table where the wines and the basket of fruit were laid for display.

I was charmed with the transformation, and was about to pick more for the bedrooms, each of which had a small, empty bud vase on its bureau, when the telephone rang. It would be someone to reserve for the night, and I ran to answer it.

"La Ferme," I said, and in my best French, "may I help you?"

"Uh. Does anyone there speak English?"

"I do." It was an American voice, I could tell.

"Swell. Look, my name is Farrell, and I'm a tour leader. Group called Foreign Junkets, know it?"

It sounded vaguely familiar. I said yes.

"I've got thirty people stranded in this place, Belan something. Our bus broke down, and it won't be ready until tomorrow, when they get the part from Nice. Can you put us up?"

I hesitated, estimating bedrooms. "How many rooms will you need?"

"Two in a room—fifteen, and a single for me."

I knew there must be at least twenty bedrooms at La Ferme, but how many were in a condition to be used I could only guess. Still, it might be the break that Conor needed. If tours would stop here, and word went abroad—

"I'm pretty sure we can," I said boldly. "And since I don't think there's another hotel around for the next thirty miles you may as well see what we can do."

"Good. See you soon."

I ran to find Conor. A truck had come up from some nursery with additional flats of flowers, and Conor was showing the man where he wanted them placed.

"Conor."

He turned.

"There was a call from Belan. A tour leader. Their bus has broken down and they need sixteen rooms for tonight. I said yes, you could put them up."

His mouth fell open. "Damn. Sophie would be away. How can we possibly—"

"They can stay at the pool while Camille and I get the rooms ready."

"You?"

"I don't mind."

"But— And lunch and dinner?"

"Berthe will manage."

"I don't like to see you doing this kind of work—"

"I don't mind. Honestly. Anyway," I said, "they're on their way, so you'll simply have to let me help."

That galvanized him. He pushed the last flat into place and hastily headed for the house with me.

At the kitchen entrance he halted and said dubiously, "You sure you know what to do?"

"I can try. All I need is the key to the linen cupboard."

His face fell. "Oh, Lord, I forgot. Sophie has it."

"Don't you have a duplicate?"

"I don't. Unless Egan made one. He might have it in his room somewhere."

We went upstairs, and then took the turret stairs at the far end. I had never been in the tower before. There were three bedrooms here, on ascending levels; we passed Conor's first, neat and bare, with the bed sheets drawn smoothly Army style over his narrow bed, a bed too narrow for lovers. I must stop thinking of Laure. Then came Mlle. Sophie's room, the door shut and locked, and last, Egan's.

"He always had romantic notions, even when he was a kid," Conor said wryly. "This was always his room."

The view down was spectacular. I thought of Bluebeard. The room was in disorder, the bed unmade, and an expensive robe tossed across a bedpost. On the dresser top were toilet articles of tortoiseshell trimmed with gold.

Conor rummaged among them, looking for the key. He opened a top drawer crammed with shirts, another with sweaters. The armoire held jackets and coats. One jacket was suede, another looked like cashmere. Conor was digging in the pockets, but he came up with nothing. He seemed not too surprised at his brother's wardrobe.

"I'll have to take the door off the hinges," Conor said curtly. "I'm going to insist on duplicate keys. I've let Sophie get away with too much."

He ran down to get some tools, and returned to work on the heavy iron hinges. Meanwhile, I had Camille open windows in all the rooms. The air smelled as stale as if no fresh breeze had penetrated in years. I pulled off rumpled, gray sheets to find unexpectedly good mattresses. I wondered: Why did the rooms that were always in use, like mine and Maria's, like Laure's, why were the mattresses thin and sloping in the middle, while the good, springy mattresses in their silky coverings were hidden under coarse sheets in disused rooms? It was as if Mlle. Sophie grudged their use . . .

In a moment I found out how right my suspicion was.

Conor called me. I went out to where he had placed the door against the wall. The interior of the closet was exposed. It was actually a small room, with inner doors as well.

"Look at this," he said in a queer voice. "I wondered where it had all gone to."

The linens that Mlle. Sophie used were on the open shelves. Behind the inner doors that were usually closed was an Aladdin's cave.

I saw stacks of bed linen with satin markers binding them. Stacks of thick towels, bath rugs. Flowered quilted spreads with draperies to match. Small rugs that looked Persian from their backs, rolled and tied and smelling of camphor. Even lamp bases, their shades shrouded in tissue paper.

"I didn't trust my memory," Conor said in the same queer voice. "I thought I had to be wrong about the house, the way it was."

Only his eyes betrayed his anger, but more than anger, hurt.

"Why should she have done it?" I whispered.

"She didn't want us to have it, that's all," he said. "She didn't want it to be used for strangers." He tightened his mouth, and looked at me. "What's the good of being angry at her? Okay, Carrie, let's forget her. Can you manage now?"

"Beautifully!"

When the first guests of Foreign Junkets appeared, we showed them where they could change into their bathing suits in the cabanas Conor had started to fashion out of the old stables. By lunchtime, Camille and I had the bedrooms ready, new drapes hung, satiny sheets on the beds beneath the new spreads, rugs replacing the soiled squares of carpet that Mlle. Sophie must have brought down from the servants' quarters on the floor above, along with the dismal mattresses and curtains.

I had found a cache of tablecloths, and we banished the threadbare white linen that hung so dispiritedly and substituted a number of pale-green and pale-rose cloths that Conor's mother must have used on the terrace tables when she and her guests dined outside. With the flowers, the room was transfigured. Conor shook his head in amazement when he saw it.

"But how the hell are they going to manage with only three bathrooms?"

"They do in English country hotels," I said. "Let's hope they just came from there. Anyway, now you'll have the money to put in bathrooms, won't you?"

He seemed suddenly to notice me for the first time. "You look exhausted, Carrie."

I felt as if I must look gray from the dust that showered me from those quilts and draperies we had removed.

"I'm going to take a quick swim, and then I'm going to help you in the dining room."

He caught my face in his hands and kissed me.

I turned away hurriedly before I gave myself away completely. He's only feeling grateful, I told myself, as I got into my bathing suit. He isn't such a fool that he doesn't guess why I want to help him, but he knows he can't accept what I am only too eager to give.

In clean pants and shirt, my hair still damp, I was just about to bring in the first trays to the dining room when a man came up to me.

"I'm Ev Farrell," he said. "You run this hotel?"

"Just helping out," I said. "The housekeeper is away for the day."

He was graying, and lined, and mopping his red face with a handkerchief, but he shook his head. "Got to hand it to whoever's running the place. Sure a pretty spot, too. How come I never heard about it before?"

Even Miss Waldron's interest in my painting had not been as richly satisfying.

"It's an old manor house, but it's only been run as a hotel for a short time." And I went on enthusiastically about La Ferme in a way that astounded me, because I would never have been able to promote my own work with anything like this fervor.

"Could use some more bathrooms," he said, interrupting me.

"They'll be in before the season is over," I said rashly.

"Sure? Because we might arrange a stopover here. The price is right. Got any material printed up on the region?"

"No—"

"Get some. Tourists like to read up on where they are. I'll give them a little in the bus tomorrow when I talk to them, but they like to have it in brochures, with maps and pictures, and excursions."

"Good idea. I'll tell Mr. Macklyn."

I went into the kitchen to tell Conor. He shook his head at me. "I don't know about those bathrooms."

"You can try. I'll try to read up on the area, and get some notes together."

"What about your painting?"

"I'll do the reading at night."

I dashed out with a tray of bread.

I was talking with some of the guests—there were a great number of schoolteachers, from Minnesota and Wisconsin— when the Citroën rattled back up the hill. I had almost forgotten about Mlle. Sophie. When I saw her stop and peer at the pool crowded with swimmers, at the rest of them stretched out on the flagged rim, sunbathing, my heart plummeted. I felt like a naughty child whose parent had just returned and discovered the disobedience.

But Mlle. Sophie disappeared inside with Egan. Maria took me aside.

"Who are these people?"

I told her. And I told her about the closet, and how Conor had to break in, and what we found. Her mouth parted.

"You're going to get it, you and Conor!"

But she was amazed at the dining room, already cleaned and ready for dinner.

"It's super, Carrie, really super! And Sophie had these linens under lock and key all this time?"

I took her upstairs to show her the rooms.

"Tomorrow when they leave we'll fix up your room and mine," I said grandly. "You can pick your own color scheme. Yellow. Rose. Green. There's enough. Did Egan ever tell you anything about Sophie to make you suspect she could do such a thing?"

"Only that she was furious about the hotel. Maybe she was hoping they would fail, and go away and leave La Ferme to her again. That's why she resents the guests. Each one is spoiling her plans."

That must be the reason, coupled with a clouded mind that could not see the reality of her position. And yet I waited like a child for the blow of her anger to fall.

All of us were needed in the dining room that night, and to help straighten up afterward, even Mlle. Sophie, who usually left the kitchen to Berthe and Camille, and there was no time to stop and think, let alone talk. We were tired when we finished, enough to want to go directly to our rooms.

Maria came into mine with me. I felt she had something on her mind.

"You do enjoy fixing up this dismal place, Carrie."

"It's a challenge," I said. "Conor seems so helpless about decoration and things like that. And I don't have that much to occupy me."

But I didn't fool her. "It's because of Conor, isn't it?"

"Why must we always get back to Conor?"

She said, "You don't want to face it. Conor doesn't want us here. He could have put the razor in the soap."

I had faced it, but unwillingly. But he was not the man who would slash a girl's dresses, unless . . . Had he defended Mlle. Sophie because he knew she was innocent?

"You see, it isn't that someone wants me . . . dead," she said. "It just means he wants to frighten me away."

That had occurred to me, too.

I said quietly, "Does Egan suspect Conor?"

"If he did, do you think he'd tell me? He'll never say a word against Conor! Any more than Conor would say anything against Egan. They're very close. The only reason Egan stays on here is because he knows how much it means to Conor to make a go of La Ferme, pay him back, and not have to feel guilty anymore."

"Wouldn't Egan keep La Ferme, if it were profitable?"

She looked down. "Egan would never be satisfied with the kind of money he could make at La Ferme. He wants to make a lot of money, fast."

"It takes more than wanting. Does he have any plans?" Outside of marrying you? She must have thought of that, herself.

She said, still not looking directly at me, "I think it's more than plans. He knows ways." She took a deep breath. "I suppose he gets tips on investments from the wealthy people he meets."

"But where would he get the money to invest? I thought neither of them had any."

She said slowly, biting a corner of her lip, "The clothes he wears have Cardin and Lanvin labels in them."

I thought of the tortoise and gold dressing set, of the vicuña robe. "Maybe they're gifts," I said carefully. "As you say, he's in a position to meet wealthy people at those hotels in the winter, and be nice to them, and maybe they give him things in return."

"You don't have to avoid saying women," she said. "I know there must be women."

I didn't answer. She was too intelligent to be put off with subterfuge.

"He never talks about women," she said. "You would think I was the only girl in his life, ever."

"I think you are, to him," I said. "I think if there ever were other women, you've wiped them clear out of his mind."

"Do you think so, Carrie?" she said, the blood coming up into her face. "Do you really think so?"

I didn't remove what weighed on her mind, maybe only lightened it a little, but after a while she uncurled from my bed and took herself back to her own room.

I undressed for bed. I was just about to reach for the bedside lamp to turn it off when there was a tap on my door. Maria?

"Come in."

In the open door stood Mlle. Sophie, still in her rusty black, her skin ashen, her mouth stretched tight, her eyes protruding.

"Thief!" she spat at me.

My first thought was, she is ill, I must quiet her; my second, she mustn't frighten the other guests. I jumped up, and tried to draw her inside so I might close the door at least, but she thrust my arms away so fiercely she bruised me.

"How dare you usurp what does not belong to you! You have allowed that canaille to use those beautiful things that are my cousin's!"

I kept my voice low and calm. "Mlle. Sophie, you weren't here this morning. I had to. There were so many people. Once they are gone you can have it all back."

"This house was not meant to entertain that riffraff! My cousin welcomed here the finest families of France! He did not intend his fine linen to be used by canaille, his fine carpets besmirched by their dirty boots! How dare you break into my closet!"

I said firmly, "I did not break in. Conor—"

"Conor!" She hissed his name. "I know what he is up to, he and his brother! They think I have no eyes and ears because I am old. They think I do not know to what use they put this hotel, this façade for their dirty business. One day I will go to the police, and they will end their lives behind bars!"

Maria appeared in the doorway, in pajamas.

"What's the trouble, Carrie?" she whispered.

Mlle. Sophie turned. *"Putain,"* she said, and darted away.

We stood transfixed, listening to her footsteps recede on the tower steps.

Maria said, "That was . . . a prostitute she called me."

"She called me a thief," I said, trying to laugh, but I was shaking.

Maria was fighting tears. "I can't tell Egan. He would be furious at her."

"Then don't," I said, taking her by the shoulders firmly and turning her around and pointing her toward her own room. I saw to it that she got into bed. She was too stricken to protest.

"We know she's crazy. You promised to pay no attention to her. So let's forget it."

She lay back. "I'm not . . . what she says, Carrie."

"Of course you're not."

"We don't even sleep together."

"You don't have to tell me, Maria. It's your affair, yours and Egan's."

"I want you to know. And it isn't my fault that we don't. It's Egan's. He won't have anything to do with me . . . that way."

I didn't know what to say. I thought. "I'm sure he's being sensible," I said carefully. "He must have very good reasons. It can't be that he doesn't want to."

"He says if it's just sex we want, it isn't going to last, and Egan says he wants it to last," she said. "He says we must be sure we want to stay together, and not just for sex."

"That sounds reasonable, doesn't it?"

"Oh, yes, very reasonable. I wish he wasn't so reasonable," she said. "It's . . . so cool. I mean, I don't like him to be so *intellectual* and all about us. I wish he'd . . . forget himself a little. I mean, if he's that in love, and all."

"Maybe it's because he thinks of you as something very special. Very precious."

Her mother might have said those very words to her. And they seemed to work, because her face slipped back into its soft lines, and she even smiled a little.

I went back to my room, brooding, not about what Maria had said, but about Mlle. Sophie. Old people lapse into fantasies, imagining terrible plots against them. Mlle. Sophie would find it easy to imagine Egan and Conor, who had usurped her domain, engaged in secret, even criminal activities. Egan and Conor both had warned us to pay no attention to her. And yet, they themselves had been affected by her words.

It was a perfect morning, hot, dry, sunny, and fragrant. It was as if the weather were conspiring, too, to show La Ferme in its best possible aspect, and the Foreign Junkets people were unwilling to leave even though the bus waited for them. They had another swim in the pool before they piled back inside.

Ev Farrell was having a final word with Egan.

"A couple of bathrooms, a tennis court, say, some fresh paint, and you'll be turning them away."

"I'll tell my brother," said Egan, looking amused.

"I'm going to bring a group in September, I'll write you the exact days. Try to get to work on those bathrooms."

Egan waved them on their way. "Poor Conor," he said to me. "His next month's work is cut out for him."

I couldn't conceive of Mlle. Sophie's words having a shred of reason to them, not with La Ferme basking in sunshine, not with Egan's wonderful smile turned on me.

But later that morning I heard them repeated.

I went back up to my room to get my painting kit. I had missed a whole day, and I had a canvas to finish. Conor was standing near the linen cupboard with Mlle. Sophie.

"I want only to borrow the key, Sophie, so I can have some others made. I can't stop to remove the door whenever you happen to be away."

"Never!" she cried. "I will not let you despoil the house any further!"

I tried to go past them unobtrusively, but she saw me.

"Perhaps you would like to give the keys to her?" she cried. "Perhaps you would like her to run the house in my place?"

"Carrie doesn't want to take over your job, Sophie," he said patiently. "She has a job of her own in New York that she'll be going back to soon."

I slipped past them as quietly as I could, hoping Sophie would ignore me. Conor's words made my heart sink. I suppose with all the unpleasantness that had come up I still did not want to think of my holiday coming to an end. Through my open door I could hear Conor continuing to argue with her, and Sophie continue to resist shrilly. Egan came running down the tower steps, and Conor called out to him: "For God's sake see if you can get through to her."

Egan said, cajolingly, "Be reasonable, Sophie dear. Suppose you should lose the key. Conor is going to damage that door if he has to keep taking it off the hinges to open it, and you wouldn't like that. You don't want any part of La Ferme spoiled, do you?"

I had to pass them again, to reach the stairs. I heard her hiss, "You cannot twist me around your finger the way you do your other women. Don't imagine for a moment that I do not see what is happening in this house. I hear the talk from your room. I am not as blind and stupid as you think." And then, breaking away from them, she called back, "Perhaps I *shall* go to the police and put an end to it all. They will come and take you both away, and that will be the last of you and the canaille that you bring here!"

I looked at them. I thought I would see exasperation, even anger, on their faces. Instead, there was dismay. Bewildered, I went out and made my way up the mountain path, my head pounding with conjectures.

They had called her cracked, obsessive, they had described her accusations as a demented old woman's ramblings, and yet they seemed almost afraid of her words. If they knew her for what she was, why did they, under cover of making light of them to us, take her words so seriously?

Why did they keep her on? Was it only because they were sorry for her? That day Maria was slashed Egan was angry enough to send her packing; what had Conor said that had made him change his mind? Were they afraid of what she would say, away from La Ferme?

One question after another.

Was the hotel a façade for some activity they wished to keep hidden? Maria and I had mentioned it jokingly the first morning we came, but we might have been more right than we knew. Conor was being driven hard for money. Egan wanted money. How far would they go to get it?

The best thing was to shut our eyes to what was going on, as long as they let us alone. In a few weeks we would be gone, and La Ferme forgotten.

And Conor, forgotten?

And Maria? We had chosen to ignore the menace in those two threatening incidents, to dismiss it as an irrational threat by an obsessed old woman. But suppose it had been more purposeful than that?

My main concern was Maria. Nothing must happen to her.

2

When I came back to the hotel in the late afternoon there were at least half a dozen cars parked in the clearing. Maria was carrying glasses from one of the tables.

"I hope we're getting a reduction on our hotel bill."

"I simply had to help, Carrie. Do you know there are fifteen people here? Isn't it fantastic? They must have seen your sign, because the first thing all of them ask about is the pool."

"Great." I tried to sound more enthusiastic than I felt.

"If Mlle. Sophie had pitched in, it wouldn't have been so bad. But she's shut herself in her room and won't come out."

"Have you tried to talk to her?"

"All of us have. Even Berthe and Camille." She added, "She hasn't eaten a thing all day."

"She'll get weak. I'll bring her a tray."

"Camille brought her some lunch, but it's still outside her door."

Egan crossed toward the salon.

"Egan!" she cried.

He turned and came back to us, looking, I thought, annoyed.

"Where were you?" she said. "I've been looking all over for you!"

"I had to go into Belan for some things. I figured I might as well pick up the frames while I was there."

"But you didn't tell me."

"Maria darling, must I tell you everything I do?"

She stared at him, speechless.

He caught himself. "I didn't want to interrupt, Maria. They couldn't have taken care of this crowd without you." He managed a smile. "Don't ever let me refer to you as the idle rich. You make a marvelous bed." He hugged her against him.

She seemed appeased. "I might have managed the time."

"Armad is coming tomorrow, with Laure. I wanted to have the painting framed so he could see it before we shipped it. Conor said he'd build the crate tonight."

She was coming again. Why should I be surprised? I knew she came every week. Maria had told me. It seemed to me that both Maria and Egan were looking at me. Did I give away my state of mind so easily? I said, "If Mlle. Sophie stays in her room tomorrow, it's going to be hard to manage."

"I'll simply have to go down to Belan and hire another girl," he said. "As long as this many people come, we can afford it. I won't have either of you working as hard as you both were these last few days. Maria has been doing a skivvy's job."

She smiled at him. "It's been fun. It's boring when you're busy."

He looked at her, smiling back, but his eyes were preoccupied. I heard her sigh, but it was almost inaudible.

"See you later!" We went upstairs together.

I passed the cupboard door and saw that it was off the hinges, so the battle lines were still drawn. The bathroom needed fresh towels and soap. I rummaged and found the little cakes of perfumed soap and put them out. She was wrong, she was hurting the hotel, hurting Conor and Egan. And yet, suppose the hotel was only a front, would Conor really care if it did not prosper? Did it matter to him at all that I had tried to help him, had I only made a further fool of myself?

I met Camille bringing down the tray from Mlle. Sophie's room. "I have carried some supper to her," she told me.

"Did she eat anything?" I gestured at the covered dishes.

"I brought her some soup, and some tea. But she ate nothing. She must be very hungry, the poor old one."

Dinner was managed competently. The lights were out in the dining room when I saw Berthe, in her hat, and carrying her basket with leftovers, wheel her bicycle toward the gate. I ran after her.

"Berthe. Perhaps you could talk to Mlle. Sophie. You've known her a long time."

She shook her head. "I tried, this morning. She cursed me. She is mad. If it were not for *les patrons* I would not stay in this house with her. Everyone in the village agrees she is crazy, to have lived here alone as she did, with hardly any food. Only the vegetables she grew, and some fruit, and now and then a little bread when M. Coudart would bring her the stale bread from the day before."

Two English boys were drinking ale on the terrace, and

they asked me to join them. We talked a little. One of them said, "Where is your friend, that pretty blond girl?"

"She's gone off for the evening, I'm afraid."

They looked incredulous. "You mean there's really some-place where one may go, for the evening?"

We laughed and I mentioned Digne, and for the tireless, Nice and Cannes. "Good Lord, at night?" one of them said.

"She's with a young man who knows the roads."

That closed all possible avenues to Maria. They went up to their room at eleven, planning an early start. Mlle. Sophie alone in her room was preoccupying my thoughts, and before I went in I walked around to the tower side of the hotel. The dim light shone from her long French windows. At least she wasn't in the dark. She was still awake.

I would speak to her. It seems to me the most dreadful aspect of life is to be cut off from communication with an-other human being. She had no one to unburden herself to, no one to whom she could release the anger boiling within her. Even if she cursed me, it would ease her, and I could bear it better than she could.

I did not like to venture up to the turret alone. It was a private enclave, apart from the rest of La Ferme, and I felt like a trespasser when I mounted the steps. There was no light from Conor's room. At the door in front of Mlle. Sophie's, the tray stood untouched, the pot of tea ice cold when I stooped and touched it. I tapped on her door.

No answer.

I tapped again. I said softly, "Mlle. Sophie, please let me talk to you."

No answer.

"Please, Mlle. Sophie, I only want to ask if I may bring you some hot soup. There is no one in the kitchen, even Berthe is gone, but she left some wonderful leek soup in the pot. I wanted to bring you some. It was especially delicious."

"Go away," was her choked reply.

"And some hot tea," I said. "It will be so much easier for you to sleep if you have something hot to drink."

I know she always carried a pot of hot tea to her room before she went upstairs to bed; the habits of the old are deeply ingrained.

There was another silence, and then her voice came, this time plaintive, conceding: "I feel a little ill. Perhaps the tea—"

Encouraged, I hurried down, warmed up the soup, boiled fresh water, and arranged a fresh tray for her. Carefully I carried it back upstairs, and tapped again.

The door opened; she stepped behind it to let me in and shut the door after me. The room was in disorder, and smelled faintly like the lair of an animal. I was ashamed of myself for my reaction. She had drawn the heavy iron shutters, and no air came in. Unwashed quilts lay heaped on the untidy bed. Mlle. Sophie was in her gray bathrobe. Her thin braids had come undone, and hung wispily, her eyes looked sore and baleful in her pasty face.

I cleared a place on a small table and put the tray down. I stirred the sugar into the cup for her. I pulled over a straight chair and led her to it and unfolded the napkin and put it over her lap. Perhaps it was my concern that reached her. She took a mouthful, and cried, "I have not enjoyed a morsel of food in this house since they came!"

"Mlle. Sophie, they don't want to hurt you. They depend on you. They want to be good to you. See how Egan drove you to the doctor—"

"So he could be with his girl."

"Even so."

Her voice was harsh. "I know they want me out. Dead would be safer. I know too much, I may be feeble, but I see everything, and my hearing is sharp."

"Why should they want you out, Mlle. Sophie?"

She was eating rapidly now, as if she were starved, and her eyes darted at me, craftily. "You know, don't you?"

"No, I don't."

She wiped her mouth, chuckling to herself. "But you are all in on it. You and that girl. The lady from Istanbul and her friends. You think I don't know? I hear through the walls."

"Mlle. Sophie, you must be wrong."

"They are rich," she said harshly. "You think they are poor, working with their hands like common laborers, grubbing in the dirt with his bare back, the older one, serving at tables like some wretched little *garçon*, with Jarret blood in him, the disgrace! But I see the letters from the bank in Switzerland—"

"Would you mind going back to your room, Carrie?"

I started, almost as much as Mlle. Sophie. Conor stood in the doorway, his face set.

"I brought Mlle. Sophie some tea—"

"I've asked you to leave. Please."

Now I was angry. He had no right to order me out after Mlle. Sophie had invited me to come in; he was arrogant, he was rude. I would not leave. I dug in my heels defiantly.

He seized my arm and yanked me out. I was too astonished to resist. Still holding my arm in a viselike grip he propelled me down the stairs.

"How dare you!" I freed my arm sharply.

"I've asked you to keep away from her."

"I brought her some tea. She'll be sick without food. Or do you want her to be sick, and die, would that be convenient for you?"

I ran back to my room. Behind me I could hear him swearing, standing still where I had left him, looking trapped and sick.

3

I had allowed my emotions to blind me to Conor, to cloud my intelligence. It was the thought I fell asleep with, the thought I woke up with the next morning. It weighed on me, it darkened the exquisite morning. I wanted only to lose myself as fast as possible in my work. I seized my painting gear and started for the stairs.

"Carrie."

It was Egan.

He lifted his eyebrows when he saw my expression. "Have I done something? You look so angry."

I managed to smile.

"Would you do the flowers, Carrie? Can you spare the time? No one does it as well."

It was blatant flattery, but I did the flowers. He stood beside me, watching me. When I had put the last flower in the bowl and was about to turn away he took my hands in his.

"This isn't like you, Carrie. You haven't lost interest in us? Because that would be awful."

I shook my head. "It has nothing to do with you."

"With Conor? I heard you last night."

So I blurted out what had happened. "So I went to her room with the tea! What harm could I possibly do?"

"Not you," he said. "But Sophie might."

I didn't answer.

He said, "What did Sophie tell you?"

"Just the same old things, over again."

He studied my face intently. "She could hurt us all because she talks wildly, and strangers might not understand."

"She can't hurt anyone who's done nothing wrong," I said shortly, thoroughly out of sorts with them all, and myself.

In my haste to escape the house I forgot to take along lunch. I wasn't hungry anyway, so I spent the day without missing it, and returned in the evening still aggrieved. Somehow I missed the usual path I took, and came out on the road but farther below toward Belan. As I trudged along I saw Egan's car off the road and almost hidden in the bushes. I could even see the back of Egan's dark head; he seemed to be talking to someone.

My first instinct was to call to him and get a lift to the hotel. My second, and more thoughtful, was to pass them as quietly as possible so that they would not even know I had seen them. If that was their hideaway, let them believe it had been undetected.

I reached the hotel and sank down on one of the terrace chairs to rest before I continued up to my room.

"Carrie?"

I looked up, startled, and saw Maria waving to me from her window. Instinctively I looked toward the parking clearing. Egan's car was not there. Maria could not have been with him.

"How did the painting go?"

I didn't answer.

"Fine." Laure's car was there. So she had arrived.

"Laure wanted to know if you'd finished any more paintings."

"No," I said briefly. "I'll be right up." It could have been someone else's Citroën; they were common enough. A glimpse of dark hair and I had automatically assumed it was Egan.

Maria's door was open, and she beckoned me in. She had new yellow draperies, and a spread with yellow roses on it, and I would have guessed she was making a greater show of enthusiasm than she really felt. She went back with me to my room to show me a new lamp Egan had found for my bedside table.

I admired it. "Where's Egan?" I said.

"Busy. And I've been too busy myself to find out." Did she say it defiantly? "There's a crowd here tonight."

"Did the Abdykians come, too?"

"Just Armad. Mme. Abdykian found the drive too much."

She lingered, while I washed at the basin.

"I helped Berthe in the kitchen today, making brains in black butter."

"You'll be an amazing cook one day."

"Even if I don't do the cooking myself," she said practically, "I can train our cook to prepare what Egan likes."

She stared at her hand. The bandage was smaller now; she chewed a corner of her lip as she studied it.

"I don't like Armad," she said. "He's always managing to bump against me, or put a hand on me."

"Have you told Egan?"

"I don't want to," she said. "I've made enough trouble since I came."

"*You've* made trouble?"

"Well, I've been the cause of it. Conor wouldn't want Laure's friends offended. You all right, Carrie?"

"Fine."

"You don't look all right," she said. "You look worried about something. Is it Mlle. Sophie?"

"Has she come out of her room? Is she eating?"

She shook her head. "It's awful, Carrie. I carried a tray up and I could hear her talking to herself. And laughing in a funny way."

"She must be getting worse," I said.

"Egan said you had a run-in with Conor over her. Is that why you're upset?"

I shrugged. "He behaved very arrogantly."

"I told you he wasn't nice, but you wouldn't believe me."

I saw Laure coming around to the terrace, in pale-custard-colored slacks and a long sweater that outlined her breasts. Mr. Abdykian followed her, looking up to our window and seeing us, and waving genially. And there was Egan, carrying the invariable shopping basket. Was it only an accident that they had met on the terrace? They were laughing and talking with animation, as if this were the first they had seen of each other.

"How was the drive?" Egan was saying. "Why don't you have a swim before dinner?"

"A wonderful idea!" cried Laure. "Tell that bad brother of yours to come out and welcome me. Where is he hiding?"

They all three vanished into the house. I looked at Maria. Her head was bent, and she continued to chew her lip as if she had forgotten I was there.

After dinner that night Egan again moved two tables together so that we could have our coffee with them, Maria and I, Laure and M. Abdykian. And again Armad brought his chair around to where its arm scraped the arm of my chair. Gallantly he poured me a brandy, his eyes never leaving me. Without the presence of Mme. Abdykian, he was proving himself even more of a nuisance.

"You have been divorced, perhaps? No? Never married? What a pity. In our country women marry young, even now. Laure was married at fifteen, is it not so?"

"I'd be an old maid," said Maria, "in your country."

"You would have been married years ago, in my country!" he cried delightedly. "The suitors would have crowded the house."

"In our country today, most girls like to finish school first," I said.

"In your country you also still have romance," said Laure. "I think it is the last country in the world where romance will die. In Europe there is much practicality. Men are older, and established in their business when they look for a wife. And they choose young girls who can bear healthy children."

"Is your husband much older?" Maria asked.

"Yes," she said. "Much."

M. Abdykian's teeth gleamed in the dark. "But still a man to be reckoned with, yes, Laure?"

She stared at him a long moment. "Did I imply he was not?"

He crooned, "I know you are Sarif's good and beautiful wife." He shrugged. "But it is a fact that we treat our wives and daughters differently than you in the United States, or even in France. Call us jealous, but I think it is different standards of honor and propriety. If Maria were my daughter, for instance, I would not permit her to travel with only the company of such a young and charming chaperone."

"M. Patrelcis allows Laure to come here alone," said Maria.

"But only to a quiet retreat like La Ferme. The mountain air is good for her nerves, is it not so, Laure?"

"It is so," she said frigidly.

"A good wife is above suspicion, besides," said Armad. "The only reason Sarif asked me to accompany her is to see that she experiences no difficulty while driving. Although I am a very poor driver myself, I am extraordinarily gifted with motors."

Laure had turned her head to stare at him. "Sarif told me it was you who asked to accompany me."

"Perhaps it was, perhaps it was," said Armad at once. "We had been talking about the long drives, and Sarif expressed his concern. I wanted to spare him the worry, so I offered to come with you."

Egan appeared, and Armad turned to him with what seemed like relief.

"Brandy, my dear boy, for all!"

"You drink too much," Laure said with distaste.

"Don't, I beg of you, sound like Anna," Armad said. "The role of scolding wife does not become someone as beautiful as you." He shrugged. "Very well, a *citron pressé* for me."

"I've put your painting in your room, Armad," Egan said. "I thought you might want to have a look at it. If you like it, and I think it came out very well, I'll see that it gets shipped out tomorrow."

Conor joined us later, and I managed to slip away to my room as soon as I could. I found it hard to pretend that all was as before between us.

But it was too early for bed. I had found a regional history in the library of La Ferme, but I didn't have the heart anymore to read it. My excitement about the project of writing up folders for tourists had died abruptly last night. I took up a piece of charcoal and began to copy the basket of fruit from the drapery material onto the whitewashed wall behind my bed. In spite of myself, I became absorbed, and soon was ready to fill in the sketch with paint. Through my open window I could hear the talk grow quieter from the terrace as one by one everyone left for bed. The silence became complete, except for the rich soughing of the branches when the wind blew. A door shut, water ran, something scudded, leaves or paper, across the gravel of the terrace.

The sound was very distinct. It was as if a flowerpot fell from an upper window. A dull, flat sound. It might even have been a bucket of water overturned onto the ground near the kitchen. Camille emptying something, if she was still up, or maybe even dropping a bundle she was carrying to the trash bins behind the shed. But I put down my brush to go to the window to look out. The terrace was dark and empty. The sound must have come from the back of the house anyway, otherwise I could have identified it more accurately.

I was sleepy now, and got ready for bed. As I started for the bathroom another sound, from the tower, arrested me. I retreated, and watched M. Abdykian move in stealthy steps from the turret stairs to his own room. He paused at his door, and glanced down the hall to my room. Stupid! Of course he had noticed the crack of light from my door. Did he know I had seen him? What reason would he have to come from the tower except to have spied on Laure and Conor? He must realize I might guess that. But why should he care if I knew? He must also realize that I would not give that information to Laure or Conor; what purpose would it serve?

But Conor should be warned. No matter what his behavior, I could not see him exposed to Laure's husband as her lover. I must have fallen asleep with this thought on my mind, because I dreamed a wild dream of Conor with a black gaping hole in his chest, saying, "It's what I deserve for losing Egan's money." And when I cried at him to go to a doctor to patch up his wound he only shook his head. "I have to finish the swimming pool," he said, hammering away at the flag-stones.

When I opened my eyes it was a gray dawn. My watch read six o'clock. A sense of foreboding lay like a weight on my chest, or maybe it was only my twisted quilt. I threw it off, and got up and dressed, and let myself quietly out of the house.

The trees dripped as heavily as if it had rained during the night, but already the sun was an apricot disk piercing through the mists to the east. Birds wheeled and swooped, scattering more drops when they settled on the branches. I stood still, and let the morning seep into me. I had become painfully alive in these last few weeks. Whether happy or unhappy did not seem to matter as much as the intensity of feeling, anxiety and fear and yearning and pleasure shaking me to my depths in a way I had never dreamed possible.

Even the silence was exciting. I did not want to break it, by going inside to take my breakfast or going back for my paint-ing gear. It would be wonderful to pick flowers with the dew on them. I had left the basket and shears at the kitchen door, so I went around to get them.

That was when I saw her. At first I wasn't even alarmed. I thought it was a heap of gray cloth on the gravel, a blanket that had been dropped from one of the upper windows. I came closer. The cobbles were stained and spotted in places, a reddish-brown. Wispy gray braids—

I didn't scream. It wasn't in my nature to scream. I would have fainted, except that the kitchen steps were near, and I managed to reach them and sit down and put my head down in my lap. It was Mlle. Sophie. I did not have to look closer to see if she was dead. The grotesquely sprawled body, the blood, the stillness— My heart began to pound now so hard it seemed to bruise my throat. When I finally tried to stand up my legs were stiff, as if with cold. I managed to walk back through the salon doors and up the stairs. The house was still asleep. I climbed the turret steps and knocked on Conor's door.

Conor opened it. He had not been sleeping; he was shaving at his washstand, and there was still soap on his chin.

When I tried to speak, my voice cracked. "Mlle. Sophie. She's lying on the ground. She's dead."

He froze.

"She must have jumped from her window. She's lying there in the kitchen courtyard."

He put down his razor and wiped his face with a towel. He seemed too shocked for speech, too stunned to act. He hung up his towel automatically, and then he seemed to see me. "Are you all right?"

I swallowed.

He took my arm and led me back to my room. "You better lie there for a while. She's in the kitchen courtyard?"

I nodded.

For a big man he moved lightly. I could hardly hear him on the steps, and only faintly the sound of the salon doors opening and closing. The sun came in with early morning fierceness, staining my room blood orange. The draperies stirred in a stray breeze, bringing in the heavy perfume of the garden. I was crying, for a deranged old woman who must have hurled herself down in a fit of irrational despondency and anger at the world, an old woman who would not be mourned or even missed.

After a while I got up and washed my face and went downstairs, overtaking Egan on the steps. He turned and smiled, but his face looked strained, as if he had not had enough sleep.

"You're up early, Carrie. I was just going for the bread."

I told him about Mlle. Sophie. He stared at me, his face mottled with color.

Conor walked in; Egan turned to him.

"I've called Dr. Froissart, and phoned the police in Digne," Conor said. "I was afraid to touch her. I just covered her with a blanket."

Egan leaned back against the wall, and shut his eyes for a moment. He said huskily, "She was just crazy enough to do something like that."

"I don't think she jumped," Conor said. "Old women like Sophie don't commit suicide."

I stared. Egan said, "What do you mean?"

"It's a feeling I have about her. She was hanging on too hard. She wanted too much to get back at us."

"Then what happened?" Egan said.

"The shutters were open, and the glass doors. She may have reached out to close them, and fell. She must have been lightheaded. She ate so little these last few days."

The windows, like all the others at La Ferme, went from floor to ceiling, and there was only the small ornamental grille as a guard. It was easy to see how she might have leaned out to grasp the handle, and lost her balance. I preferred to believe it, rather than that she was driven to suicide. My mind stops in horror, unable to comprehend the profound-ness of despair that would make anyone kill himself.

Most of the guests left before they even knew of the body lying in the courtyard. And if they had known, they wouldn't have lingered, even out of curiosity. They were on vacation, the day was hot and fine and the Mediterranean waited less than two hours away. It was an old servant who fell, yes? Poor creature, to die on such a fine day, and off they would rattle in their little cars, their luggage bouncing under the green plastic covers laced to the roofs.

Armad and Laure slept late, wakened by the arrival of the police car and a van. They appeared, expressed shock, and asked for their breakfast. Egan had told Maria. She came down with him, looking white and frightened and very like a child.

"It's horrible, isn't it, Carrie? And for you. You found her." She sucked in her breath.

"Maria," I said. I had been thinking this ever since I had been left alone that morning. "Do you think it might be a good idea if we left La Ferme? We might travel for a while and then—"

"Oh, *no*, Carrie! I would never leave Egan!"

She made me feel I was mad to imagine she would even consider the idea.

Camille and Berthe watched the scene in the courtyard from the kitchen windows. They were excited to be present; this would go into the folklore of Belan-les-hauts, and they would be catapulted into importance. They couldn't be ex-pected to grieve: Mlle. Sophie had been demented; it was all for the best, poor old soul.

The officer in charge came into the kitchen and made a

place for himself at the table where he could question us. He wrote down what each of us said, and asked us to initial our statements after we had read them.

Camille and Berthe tapped their foreheads several times when they were called to speak, so I knew what they were saying even if I couldn't follow their rapid French.

Conor, waiting with us in the hall, said, "I'm going to tell him about the cupboard, and her locking herself in and refusing to eat."

"Why not?" Egan shrugged.

Laure's and Armad's interviews were brief; they only knew Sophie to bring an extra towel or, grudgingly, an additional pillow. They spoke with a restrained arrogance, as if they had already wasted too much time on the matter.

When it was my turn, I told as well as I could how Mlle. Sophie had acted toward us. Yes, I really thought she was distraught and had fancies, yes, she had eaten only a little soup and tea for two days, yes, I thought she had fallen, the hinges were stiff and rusted, it was easy to imagine how it happened.

The inspector took down the names and addresses of those guests who had departed; perhaps he might trouble to look them up for a statement, but I had a feeling he would not. Mlle. Sophie's room was gone over methodically, the windows and other surfaces dusted for fingerprints, but the inspection was routine and cursory, and no one doubted for an instant that it was an accident. The body was driven away in the van for an autopsy, and her room locked in case any further investigation was necessary.

Laure left with Armad almost immediately.

"It has taken the heart out of my holiday," Laure said with a wan smile.

I wondered why she would not choose to stay a little longer near Conor, who looked grim and was even more silent than usual, but perhaps she was afraid of the police and the newspapers which might carry the story.

In the lull after the police left and before the evening guests arrived we four sat in the salon.

"We'll have to find a housekeeper to take Sophie's place," Egan said. "I won't have Maria working as hard as she has. Look at her, she's pale. What will your aunt think of us if you go home looking as if you haven't even had time for the sun?"

Maria did look pale. She said, "Honestly, I don't mind. I haven't anything else to do."

I said, "Why not let Camille be housekeeper? She seems very efficient."

"And bring another girl up from the village. An excellent idea, Carrie," Egan said. He turned to Conor.

But Conor was deep in his own thoughts, and seemed to wrench himself back to us. "What? Sure. Will you take care of it, Egan?"

He got up and walked outside. I put aside my pride and followed him. He seemed so completely alone. I found him in the courtyard, staring down at the cobblestones where Sophie's body had lain.

He started when I came up to him.

"Carrie."

"It does no good thinking about it now."

"I know." And then, as if it had been on his mind all this time, "I'm sorry I acted that way with you in her room. I thought you were just encouraging her to go off the deep end."

"I only wanted to let her know we were worried about her."

"She was irresponsible, and she hated you. She might have even attacked you."

"I wasn't afraid of her."

He looked away. Then, changing the subject abruptly, he said, "Did you hear anything the night she died?"

I told him about the sound I thought I had heard, the sound that might have been Sophie's body striking the ground. He should have heard it too, his room was right below hers, but Laure had been with him that night, so I suppose his windows were closed and the shutters drawn. That reminded me of Armad. "Armad was on the tower steps that night."

"When?" He shot the question at me.

"It was . . . after."

He stared at me.

I said, "I saw him once before, too. The last time he was here. He was walking up the stairs very quietly. And he stayed out of sight for a while before he came down."

His eyes were still fixed on my face, frowning.

"I think he was spying on you and Laure," I said.

Blood flamed in his face. He said huskily, "Have you told this to anyone? To Maria?"

I shook my head.

He put his hands on my arms. "Keep it to yourself. Will you do that?"

"Of course, if—"

"It's important. For your sake as much as anyone's," he said, and left me.

4

It was a week later before the police released Mlle. Sophie's body to Conor and Egan. The examination had shown that her death had been due to a broken neck, the result of a fall from her window, possibly due to a stroke. The funeral was held in the church in Belan; except for Conor and Egan, Maria and I, Camille and Berthe, only a few people in the village remembered Sophie enough to attend the service, and only the six of us walked behind the hearse in a pitifully small procession to the cemetery.

When we drove back to La Ferme, we found the first guests had already arrived, and Jeanne, the new girl hired to help Camille, had shown them to their room. It was like an omen, marking a new period for La Ferme.

Maybe it was only because it was August, the beginning of the holiday season for most of France, when even the byroads like the one that went through Belan-les-hauts were crowded, but all at once it seemed that at least half the bedrooms at La Ferme were always filled.

Mlle. Sophie's death seemed to lift a black veil from the hotel. Now there were Camille and Jeanne moving briskly in their white aprons, ample linen, a profusion of flowers. Conor had taken over an unused sewing room, a second floor pantry, and the smallest of the bedrooms, and was converting them into bathrooms. A man from the village came to help him, and in a week he was ready to lay the tile for the floors.

And yet if the black pall seemed to have lifted from La Ferme, none of us there felt entirely free of it. Egan, who was the most carefree of us all, often seemed withdrawn, and that tender, amused expression in his eyes that had charmed me so on our first meeting appeared less and less often. Maria was more bewildered by the change in him than affected by Sophie's death, I think. At least Conor had his work as refuge; he tackled his pipes and fittings as if it were possible to sweat away her memory in the August heat. When Laure returned to La Ferme for her weekly visit I thought I even saw a change in her. She was quieter, and seemed less interested in making a display of herself.

I know it was more than my imagination. How could we not be affected? I paused in my painting often, remembering those pitiful gray braids snagged on the cobbles. Maybe it was dissatisfaction in our minds as to how and why she died, maybe it was a sense of guilt, for having failed another human being.

One morning Conor stopped me as I was leaving for the day.

"I have to drive into Nice to pick up some tiles for the bathrooms," he said. "I thought—you're good at this sort of thing. It would be a help if you came along."

I came along.

It was another in a chain of flawless days. The road twisted up one side of the mountain and spiraled down the other, and when it seemed as if the mountains would stretch on forever, the Mediterranean spread across the horizon like a pale mirage, swimming in a haze of heat. I made a sound of surprise and pleasure, and Conor pulled over to the side of the road so I could look longer.

Up to now we had spoken very little, but the silences were comfortable. Often silences between people who knew each other as slightly as Conor and I are strained, and I am the sort who searches frantically for something to fill them. I felt no need today, nor did he, apparently. We sat companionably and stared at the sea.

"I'm glad we got away," he said. "Sometimes I feel I'm in a cage there. Whichever way I turn, bars stopping me."

"It's a pity you can't enjoy it more," I said. "La Ferme could be so beautiful. Even now it seems to be coming out of itself, losing that shabby, musty look."

"Thanks to you."

"Oh, no. I've just touched the surface. It's all your work."

"I wouldn't mind the work if I didn't feel the . . . urgency. I feel someone's on my back, I can't stop to look around."

"I think that's awful! It's *wrong.*"

He said, wryly, "Among a lot of other things."

I was sure he meant his relationship with Laure, so full of tensions and uncertainties, but I could not discuss Laure with him. There was also Egan.

"You've always shouldered too much of the blame for Egan," I said. "I don't even think he needs to be worried over as much as you do. I can't help feeling that Egan will come out all right without you. People like Egan generally do."

"You believe that?"

I nodded.

"You told me yourself about your stepfather. He had no money when he married your mother, but they seem to have been very happy."

"He was very like Egan," he said. "A charmer."

"You're blaming yourself for influencing him, but he grew up in that pattern, with your stepfather. He grew up in a home where a man felt no discomfort taking money from a woman, and living a carefree life because of her."

He listened, but maybe he was only saying to himself how like an earnest schoolteacher I sounded. And then he smiled at me, which was rare enough for me to notice. "Now that you've cheered up La Ferme, are you trying to do the same for me?"

"I'd like to."

He looked at me soberly. The look lengthened. He is going to kiss me, I thought, feeling a pounding in my throat. But his mouth tightened, and he turned away, and started the motor. "We'd better get started."

I felt cheated. There's Laure, I told myself, staring out the side window so he could not see my expression, and you guessed right in the beginning that he would be the kind of man who would find deception difficult.

Nice lay before us, crowded, white plaster dazzling in the sun, the unfamiliar noises of traffic, the smell of hot tar and gasoline and salt water. Along the Boulevard des Anglais the palm trees bent in the strong hot wind that carried with it the voices from the beach, the shouts of children, the noisy surf. Banners and awnings flapped on the cabana clubs and eating places. The Promenade was crowded with strollers; across from it the hotels lined up, concrete and glass and steel, an international architecture. Only when we turned into the old city of narrow streets did I feel gratefully that I was back in France. We parked opposite the tile factory and went inside.

It took very little time to pick out the patterns. Conor leaned toward the dark-red tile that covered the bedroom floors at La Ferme. I was captivated by the flowered and scrolled tiles that came from Italy. Conor acceded at once.

"You're trying to turn that old derelict into a bower of roses," he said. Again his look lingered on me, until I found it difficult to return casually. "I can imagine what your apartment in New York must be like."

What was my apartment in New York like? Not a flower. Clean and cool, like me, before I came here. How could I ever go back?

We found a restaurant along the old port and ordered bouillabaisse and wine. The sun and wine affected us both. We laughed together. Once he reached over and roughed my hair. I don't know what I said to make him do it.

There were bright-flowered cushions on the chairs we sat on. "These would look beautiful on your terrace," I said.

"More flowers?"

"And even more. How about whitewashed tubs of geraniums and petunias scattered as a border?"

"Flowered umbrellas over the tables?"

When we left the restaurant we held hands, walking back to the car. The touch of his work-hardened hand made me curiously breathless. We lingered, browsing in shopwindows; I stared at our reflection, at our joined hands, as if I wanted to print it on my mind. I found a lovely wicker birdcage at an open stall, and insisted on bringing it back with us.

"We don't have a bird for it."

"We'll get one. A bright-green parrot."

"To go with the petunias?"

Reluctantly we got into the car, as if we knew we could not hold onto the feeling we shared. We drove through the city, we turned up into the mountains. The air grew cooler and fresher as we climbed. When we reached the top of one hill he stopped. I looked at him in surprise.

He said, "I thought you might want a look back at where we were."

We both got out, and came together on the dusty shoulder of the road, thick with asters and small wild red poppies. His arms went around me so easily it was as if we had done this many times before. I held him as tightly as he held me. I thought of Egan and Maria that first night we came, and how thirstily they kissed. It seemed as if ours was the same, and I had the same thickening in my throat, the same stinging in my eyes.

When he let me go he said huskily, "Damn that place. I wish we didn't have to go back."

And Laure? *Laure?*

"Carrie," he said, "this is no good for us. I was wrong to let it start."

"*Why?*" But I knew why. Laure.

His mouth hardened in that line I'd begun to fear.

"There isn't anything I can say."

He opened the door for me with finality. I slid in. He did not start the motor up immediately but frowned ahead of him. "Carrie," he said, "I'd like you to go home. Take Maria and get out of here."

It was the last thing I had expected him to say.

"But why? Don't you want me here?"

"No. Yes, you know I do. But not the way things are. I don't know what's going to happen. It's the best way. Go now."

I waited until I was more sure of my voice. I said, "I'll speak to Maria."

It was not the way I had imagined the day would end. I was too hurt, too shaken, to even remember the way it had begun.

V

1

SOMETIMES I AM APPALLED by how much our lives are directed by coincidence. There is a mindlessness to coincidence, that reduces one to powerlessness, that casts doubt on even the small part one plays in controlling one's destiny. If my father had not explained rocks and flora to Miss Waldron I might never have joined the staff of the Burns Junior College; if I had not taught Maria art I might not have come to La Ferme and met Conor. Or come near death in the twenty-eighth year of my life, but that was later . . .

And if Maria had not had a sore throat I would not have stayed at the hotel that morning and seen the postal truck arrive with the crate. If she had not had the sore throat and Egan had not been alone that morning, he might not have stayed away as long as he did to repair the Citroën's exhaust, and might have taken the crate himself. Well.

When I stopped in at Maria's room to see if she wanted to have breakfast with me, she complained that her throat was sore. Her cheeks seemed flushed when I touched them. In our medical kit under "Sore Throat," I found listed an antibiotic and a lozenge, and instructions to call a doctor if the fever was high. The thermometer read one hundred and one, and she wasn't uncomfortable, so she took the medicine as prescribed and asked for her breakfast tray in bed.

Her hunger was a reassuring sign. I left her to Egan, who breakfasted in her room with her, and went down and ate mine on the terrace, and then instead of going off, I stayed behind, to be on hand in case she needed anything.

When Egan left for Belan I sat with her. She asked me to paint the same kind of fresco on her wall as I had on the one in my room. It would amuse her to watch me, so I picked out the design of an old candleholder she had on her bureau and sketched it on the wall above it. It showed two aristocratic white dogs leaning above a shield with fleur-de-lis, a gold crown above them, and below them the words *Da Viken*, which might be Breton, and whose meaning I hoped was auspicious.

"You like it here, don't you?" Maria said.

"It could have been perfect, if . . . if not for Sophie." That was not the way I would have finished the sentence, honestly. "Don't you like it?"

"It isn't the way I imagined the summer," she said, her voice thickening.

"Why don't we go home?" I said. "We can come back next summer, when everything will be different." It wasn't the first time I had broached the idea to her since Conor had asked me to take her and leave, but she refused even to listen, and I suppose my words were halfhearted by now.

"You know I won't leave Egan," she said, turning her face away.

"You're not very happy, are you, Maria?"

She didn't answer right away, as she might have once. And then she said. "It's awful to be in love, and not be sure."

"Aren't you sure?"

"Sure of me," she said thickly. "But I'm not sure of him."

"You don't think he loves you?"

"I don't *know*."

I outlined the dog's collar with care. It's awful to be in love and not be sure. To be in love with no reassurance at all, now that is really awful. To be in love and be told to go home, that is awful, too.

"He's *different*," Maria said. "He's always thinking of something else, even when we're together."

I finished the other collar, and started on the crown.

"I feel *old*," Maria whispered. "Nothing is simple anymore."

The telephone was ringing downstairs. In a moment Jeanne came up to call me. It was Egan on the phone in Belan.

"How's Maria?"

"She seems comfortable enough."

"The car needs a new exhaust, and the garage here doesn't have one to fit. They phoned Digne, and they have one there, so if everything is quiet and you don't need me, I'll take a run over to Digne and get it fixed. Will you explain to Maria? Tell her I'll bring her a surprise if she's a good girl."

"I'll tell her."

I was on my way to the stairs again and, passing the open front door, saw M. Fresny of the post office mounting the steps carrying a large crate. I stopped to let him in. He leaned the crate against the wall.

"It was returned this morning by the Landon company

that handles the freight. Something fell on it in transport, they are desolated, and although they could repair the crate themselves they wish you to check the contents again to make sure there has been no damage. Naturally, they will pay if any damage has been done since they acknowledge it is their fault—"

Through the broken slats I could see the crate contained what looked like the two paintings Egan had shipped out. Sure enough, there was Maria Waldron's name and address on Madison Avenue in New York printed on the label.

"Thanks, M. Fresny. I will look over the paintings myself."

I carried them upstairs to Maria's room, but when I saw that she was asleep I continued on to my own room and propped the crate on a chair. With a knife I always keep in my painting gear I began to pry off the broken slats. The paintings themselves were encased in heavy cardboard within the crate, and placed front to front to protect the face of the canvasses, but I could see that the cardboard had been staved in by whatever had dropped on it, and so using the knife I cut away the cardboard as well.

Cutting the cords that held them together, I carried one of the paintings to the window to examine it carefully. The back of the canvas seemed untouched, but I wanted to see if any of the paint itself had flaked off. It looked unmarred. I ran my finger along the gold leaf of the frame to see if any of the gold had been chipped; the carpenter in Belan could repair it before Egan had the paintings crated again. My finger found the broken place before my eye spotted it. It was at the corner, just where the moldings were mitered together, a small piece about an inch long missing. The chip must have fallen to the bottom of the crate; I could find it, and glue it back on. I felt in the crate, and there it was.

It was mitered at one corner and smooth at the other, whorled on top where the gold leaf was applied, smooth on the bottom where it had been glued.

I stared at it. The molding must have been pieced, because the smooth side opposite the mitering also had traces of glue on it. The carpenter must have cut one molding too short and had to piece it, and it was this piece that had fallen out.

Still, it wasn't characteristic of such precise and finished work. If the carpenter had made a mistake, he would have discarded the strip of molding and used another, without its being such a great loss.

Unless he had cut all the moldings too short, and then decided he would piece them rather than discard them. I examined the frame again, and again it was my fingers rather than my eye which detected the seam on the other end of the molding as well. And there was that faint, almost indetectable line at each end of every molding. Now I took out the other painting and examined it the same way, but here there seemed no break at all. It was only on Armad's painting that the moldings had been pieced.

I still had no real comprehension of what I was uncovering, and yet I was driven to go on.

My fingers were suddenly unsteady. I pried off the entire strip with my knife and carried it to the light. The edge that had been pieced was covered with a film of dry glue. I scraped that away with the knife. Underneath the glue was a round wooden plug, about an inch and a half in diameter, cut from the molding itself. I stopped and took a deep breath, and inserted the tip of my knife so I could free the plug. It fell out on my lap. I pushed a finger into the hollow, and felt something soft.

I ran to get my tweezers. Using them carefully, I pulled out a transparent glassine bag. It contained white powder.

I don't know what I thought I would find. I don't know what I imagined might lie behind the façade of La Ferme, but the last thing in my mind was this. It must be heroin. Once I had been called in about a student in my class, and questioned. They had found a small paper of powder on her that looked just like this, and it was heroin. I stared at the tube in my hand for a long time before I dropped it as if it were a snake. What should I do now?

And then, because I did not know what else to do, I proceeded to loosen the other three strips of molding, prying out the plugs and pulling out three more plastic, or glassine, tubes.

"Carrie?"

Maria's voice sounded stronger through the wall. I pushed the tubes frantically into my top bureau drawer and ran to her room.

"It wasn't *that* urgent," she said, and began to laugh at me. I don't know what she saw on my face, but it might have reflected the chaos of my thoughts. "I just wondered if you were still around."

"Want anything? It isn't time yet for another pill. Something to drink?"

"I still have the pitcher of orangeade," she said, sitting up and pouring herself some. "I think I'm better."

"But stay in bed today anyway," I said, forcing myself to talk coherently. "Until your fever is gone."

"Okay," she said contentedly. "Give me that book over there, will you, Carrie?"

I handed it to her.

"Egan back yet?"

I remembered his call with a wrench. "He called before. He's going to have the exhaust taken care of, in Digne. He said he'll bring you a surprise if you're good."

Her eyes shone. "Did he really?"

I nodded. "Well . . . If you don't need me, I . . . got started on something in my room—"

"You go ahead," she said, settling back against her pillow.

At least the interim had given me a chance to order my thinking. First of all, I must put the frames together again. Instinctively I sensed that I must hide my discovery.

I ran down to the shed where Conor kept his tools, and found glue in a drawer. I paused. Hanging on the wall were all sizes of augers, bits, and braces, available to anyone who wanted to hollow out a piece of molding. Armad could have come down, found the tool he needed, and done the work in his room at night without being detected. Egan had left the painting in his room before it had been crated.

I mustn't be found here, even though I could come up with several reasons for needing the glue. I hurried back to my room and feverishly got to work regluing the molding to the frame. To do it properly, the glue had to dry before the pieces could be put on. I was in an agony of impatience. Egan would be coming home soon.

I remembered, and ran to lock the door.

At last the moldings were on again, and looking as if they had never been disturbed, at least at first glance. Suppose someone suspected the frames had been tampered with? Suppose Armad were to hear about the crate coming back to us, and would decide to inspect the frames himself?

I caught myself. Always Armad. Because he was a perfumed, oily man with unpleasant manners, it had to be Armad. But suppose it were Laure. Or Egan? Or Conor?

It was Conor who was expert with tools. It was Conor who made the crate. It was Conor who wanted desperately to return the money he had lost to Egan.

I couldn't imagine how much money the four tubes were worth, but it didn't matter. Large sums of money were involved. This was not the first shipment, probably, and probably there would be others. Was this Conor's secret, and why it was sealed within him, and was this why he wanted me to get away before something should go wrong? Was this the hell he was afraid would break loose? Was it only that he didn't want me to find out what kind of crime he was engaged in, or did he want to shield me from involvement?

My hands ran over the moldings, and this time they were even more unsteady. Some more gold leaf was needed, where it had chipped along the edges. I did not dare go down again. I had a small jar of gold paint in my kit. It wasn't gold leaf, true, and later on it would darken and the difference would become visible, but it would have to do. I rubbed it with a rag in all the seams.

Someone was tapping on my door. "Carrie?"

Egan.

"Yes?" Thank heaven the door was locked.

"May I come in?"

Did he know? Had he met M. Fresny in the village and had the postman told him of handing the crate to me?

"Just a minute." The gold paint was too fresh to risk letting him see the paintings, if I were to come out with it and tell him that I had opened the crate to inspect the canvasses. I looked around frantically. The door of the armoire was open.

Making no sound, I carried the crate and the canvasses and the wrappings to the armoire and closed the door on them. Then I unlocked the outside door.

His eyes went past me to the painting kit lying open on the bureau.

"Working? I don't want to disturb you. But Maria is asleep and I wondered how she was feeling."

He couldn't know about the crate. His face looked just the same, just as it had since Sophie's death, the skin a little tighter over the fine bones of his face, maybe, the eyes too tired for someone so young. Of course, he might be dissimulating. Armad? Laure? Egan? Conor? Could they all be in it together?

He was looking at me strangely now, and I knew *I* was no expert at dissimulating. I brought myself back with an effort. "Maria? I'm sure she'll be feeling lots better when she wakes up."

"Are *you* all right?" he said.

I made myself smile. "I've been working with such concentration for a few hours that I'm sort of dazed."

He smiled at that, too. "But you're not worried about Maria?"

"Of course not. If I were, we'd call Dr. Froissart, or even drive her into Digne. She only has a mild sore throat, and she was feeling more like herself even before she went to sleep."

"Carrie—"

I saw suddenly that there was something he wanted to say, but was finding it difficult. He was so close that I could see the grain of his skin, the transparent gray irises, the dark arch of his brows, I could smell his hair, and I felt a strange communication of the ecstasy Maria must feel, of the delight they

had in each other. Egan had to be innocent. It was as important to me that it not be Egan as it was that it not be Conor.
My mind darted to alternatives. Egan might serve the criminals unwittingly. Armad might be using him. Egan had put
the framed painting in Armad's room overnight. Armad had
opportunity to drill the frames through, to insert the glassine
tubes. Egan, unsuspecting, would send it off to Miss Waldron's address, that most impeccable name and address that
had once belonged to an ambassador and to a United States
Senator before it became Maria's. I remembered the velvet
jewelry box Egan had sent to Maria, for a friend; had there
been heroin concealed in that, too?

"You are worried," Egan said. "If it isn't Maria's sore
throat, what is it? I might be able to help."

I shook my head. "Nothing. Just a brown study."

"Carrie, I did come here to say something. I know you're
not just keeping an eye on her. I know she means a great deal
to you."

I nodded.

"I'm glad you're here, for both our sakes. So you can see
how it is, with us. I want you to see. I want you to believe
how much she means to me."

My heart cramped painfully. Why was he telling me this,
now? If those glassine bags were in some way connected to
Egan, it meant total disaster for them, for their dreams of a
future together. It was inconceivable. Maria would know it,
somehow. She could not love someone involved in so vicious
an affair.

"She is all I've ever cared about," he said. "I know it would
be hard to believe, to a cynic. I don't think you are a cynic,
Carrie. But she is rich and I am not, and— Carrie, I could
have had money before. A lot of it. Not as much as Maria's,

maybe, but all I could ever need. There are a great many women with a great deal of money in the part of the world I frequent. I wouldn't say it to you, except that it's so important to me that you understand."

"I do understand, Egan."

"I want to marry her," he said. "She's very young, and I am sure her guardian would disapprove, but I don't want to lose her. You could help us. If you understood."

"You're coming to New York, Maria tells me. You'll have a chance to talk to Miss Waldron. I will do whatever I can to help Maria, and you—"

"Egan? Are you talking to Carrie?" Maria's voice was still drowsy with sleep.

"Be there in a moment, darling." He took my hand and kissed it. "Thanks, Carrie."

He had in his other hand a round red velvet box with a black bow on it.

"Chocolates," he said. "They can't hurt her, can they?"

I shook my head, and he went into Maria's room, and I went back to mine. I took the crate and paintings from the armoire, tied the cardboard back on with the pieced lengths of cord, and fitted the paintings back into the crate. It looked almost exactly as it had when M. Fresny had delivered it.

I opened the door. No one was in sight. Hurriedly, I went out into the hall, trying to make no sound as I passed Maria's room, holding the crate against me. I managed to get down the stairs unobserved, and leaned the paintings against the wall beside the door where M. Fresny had originally left them.

"Carrie?"

I started violently.

Egan was looking down at me from the landing above.

"Maria says she'll have some lunch. Would you mind asking Jeanne to bring up a tray?"

"Of course. One for you, too?"

But his glance had shifted; I saw him looking at the crate. "What's that?"

I made a point of looking behind me. "Oh. That's the crate of paintings you sent out. M. Fresny brought it back awhile ago. Something fell on it in the shipping, and a few slats were damaged, and they wanted us to see if the paintings were all right. I examined the cardboard, but it's just pushed in, so I'm sure the canvasses weren't touched." How irreversible a lie is. "It slipped my mind to tell you."

His voice was thoughtful. "Strange that I didn't notice it when I came in."

Panic had made me lie. If I'd had time to think. I might have said that I'd gone over them and they were untouched, and he might have thought nothing more about them.

2

I stayed with Maria a good part of the day, grateful to her for distracting me with her talk. Her spirits were high. That round velvet box of chocolates was a talisman to her; when she kept opening it and offering it to me it was as if she wanted to share something rare and precious.

I finished the painting on her wall, which made my distractedness understandable to her. Distractedness was a mild word. Those glassine tubes in my drawer seemed to me as volatile as nitroglycerin.

Whom could I talk to? Not Maria. She would be angry at me for prejudging Egan, as indeed I had, along with the others. She wouldn't believe me even if it were so, if Egan denied it. Not Egan: I knew I could not talk to Egan. Then Conor.

If it were Conor who was involved, I don't think he would deny it. He might ask me not to give him away, though; I could see him doing that. But not lying. And then I would be torn between love and conscience.

But first and foremost, the drugs would have to be destroyed. That much I would see to.

Maybe I could get Conor to agree to destroying the drugs as the price of my silence. I might even exact from him a promise to have nothing further to do with such traffic, again. I was too naïve to realize how foolish my reasoning was, but then what understanding did I have of crime, or the thought processes of criminals? If Conor were a criminal, there would be no room in his mind for sentiment. He would be concerned with the threat to his own life, and I was the sole source of that danger.

I had dinner with Maria in her room. The dining room worked smoothly with Camille in charge; she was a minor tyrant and could exact marvelous efforts from Jeanne, ordering her about with her newly assumed authority. Egan was free early, and came up to stay with Maria. I went down to the terrace and had a brandy. I felt I needed it. Those glassine tubes in my bureau drawer: Should I destroy them and say nothing, and hope that no one would ever discover at this end that the frames had been tampered with? Once we were safely back in New York we were out of danger. When the loss was discovered, there would be no reason to believe I had anything to do with it. Some zealous inspector might have spent some time on them, and even uncovered the heroin himself.

Conor crossed the courtyard toward the shed, carrying the

crate. I watched him. Best to say nothing, I told myself. Destroy the heroin and say nothing. I don't know what made me get up and follow him.

He already had the broken slats pried off when I came in.

"The express company must have had these off already," he said. "The nails practically came out in my hand."

I should have confessed my part in it then and there. I should have realized I would have difficulty in lying to him. Instead, I tried to invent a pretext that brought me to the shed.

"I came here to . . . to speak to you. You asked us to leave. I thought you should know . . . Maria won't hear of it. I can't leave her here, and go home alone."

I suppose he heard the agitation in my voice. He looked at me for a moment, and then he turned back to the crate. "I can't force you to get on a plane."

"Is it that we are . . . getting in your way? Is that why you want us to go?"

Again his glance was searching. He must have detected something odd in my manner.

"It's very important that I know," I said.

That ready flush came up into his face as it always did when he was moved. "If . . . things were different, I'd want nothing more than for you to stay. You must know by now that you're the only good thing that has happened to me."

I met his eyes. I was wordless. I didn't want him to say any more. I wanted only to remember his words, and the way he said them, if I took nothing else back from La Ferme. I knew I had to tell him the truth, then.

"I opened the paintings before, myself."

He said, "Why didn't you say so?"

"I didn't know whether or not to tell you."

"Why not?" he said. "I don't understand."

If it were Egan's face I was looking into I would have wondered what lay behind those long gray eyes. But Conor's was not designed for deceit; it was too blunt, too exposed.

Maybe if I didn't still hear those words ringing seductively in my ear I might have asked myself why his face was so still as he questioned me.

"Because," I heard myself say, "I found something."

His hand held the hammer tight, so that his knuckles were white on the handle.

"A section of the molding had fallen off," I said. "I was going to glue it back on but then I saw that it had been glued before—" I stopped.

"Go on," he said curtly.

"I couldn't help but notice. There were channels drilled in the moldings, all four sides."

I saw with despair that his face had hardened.

"It was heroin," I said. "Four glassine bags like long tubes, to fit inside the moldings."

The silence lengthened.

"Did you put them back?"

"No. They're in my room."

His face had formed into grooves and ridges I had never seen on it before. He stared at the crate he held, his whitened knuckles still gripping the hammer.

"Well," he said dryly, "I better close this up."

Moving automatically, his head down, he selected two identical pieces of wood from a stack of several the same size. I suppose he had cut them all at once when he had built the crate. With a few deft strokes he nailed them on.

"That should do it," he said without expression, standing

the crate against the wall. "Egan can take it down to the post office in the morning."

His eyes looked sore and dry.

He said, "Did you tell anyone about this?"

"Nobody."

He expelled his breath.

"I'd like to see those tubes."

"I'll go up and get them."

"It might be better if I went up to your room with you."

He shut the shed door behind us and we went back to La Ferme. Only a few people lingered on the terrace; lights shone in several bedrooms. There was still one burning in Maria's. When he followed me into my room he took the precaution to lock the door behind him.

The tubes of heroin were still in my bureau drawer where I had left them. I'd been too distraught even to conceal them.

I handed them to him. "They are heroin, I suppose."

He did not answer right away, and then briefly nodded. "Have you thought of what you are going to do with them?"

"I thought . . . I would destroy them."

"Did it occur to you that you might go to the police?"

I met his eyes. I said steadily, "I guess I haven't had a chance to think it through. My first thought was to destroy them."

He said, "Let me have them. I'll put them in the furnace."

I remembered my notion that I would exact a promise from him, in return for my silence, and I realized what I should have known before, how completely naïve and unrealistic I was. I was now in his hands as much as he was in mine.

I don't know how clearly my thoughts were mirrored in

my face, but they must have been. Dryly, he said, "Do you trust me to destroy them? You can watch if you want."

"I don't want to."

He studied me. "You know what position this puts you in?"

"I can imagine."

"You had better know it," he said, his voice roughening. "I don't know how much these bags represent, but it means a much larger operation, other shipments. Other men. A great deal of money."

"Conor, will you tell me who is behind it?"

He said deliberately, "I will not, I *would* not, even if I knew. And I don't know. For your own sake. You're already too much involved for your safety. I warn you, Carrie, keep absolutely quiet about what you found. If you let on to anybody about it, you're in serious danger."

I said, my mouth dry, "I won't tell anybody."

"Now do you understand why you have to take Maria and get away, fast?"

But he had warned me long before, before I'd stumbled onto the heroin. Is this what he was afraid would happen, is this what he did not want me to find out? Then he had always known about it. There was a lead weight on my heart. I managed to say, "I'll never get Maria to leave, not unless I tell her everything. And even then she might not go. She would have to be convinced Egan was involved."

"Egan?" he said sharply. "How is Egan tied in with this?"

I was confused. "I didn't say he was. Only that it would be the only reason Maria might consent to leave, and even then I wouldn't be sure." I stopped. I said, "Egan picked out the frames."

"And I crated them. And any number of people had access to them. Someone in the carpenter's shop, maybe."

I nodded dumbly.

"This isn't Egan's style," he said. "You don't know him. Egan can get money in his pocket much more easily."

Why was he defending Egan so forcefully?

"I'll take these," he said abruptly. "Good night."

He pushed them into his jacket and let himself out.

He had scarcely closed the door behind him when I heard him say: "Egan? You still up?"

"I've been keeping Maria company."

Their footsteps receded toward the tower. Egan had been in Maria's room. Her light had been on before. He could not possibly have heard what we said through the thick walls, only the muffled sound of our voices. Would Conor's being with me in my room make him wonder? But why should it? He may even have guessed my feelings about Conor if Maria had not given me away, and I was sure she had. Unless he had become suspicious about me since he had seen the crate appear suddenly in the downstairs hall, and I might have acted guilty. And then Conor's presence in my room—

No, I was bumbling around in the dark now. Someone could be using Conor, someone like Laure. If she and Armad were involved together in the conspiracy to ship drugs, whom would she turn to more easily than Conor for help? If he loved her, how could he refuse her?

I thought of Sophie. She had hinted that both Conor and Egan had more money than they let on to; there was no need for either of them to work as common laborers, she had said. She had talked of letters from a bank in Switzerland.

Maria knew something. Her preoccupation was more than

her slashed hand, her ruined dresses. She was worried about Egan. She would never betray him even if she knew, just as I would be unable to turn Conor over to the authorities.

My head ached, and I pressed my cold fingers to my temples. Conor had said I was the best thing that had ever happened to him. Had he said it to ensure my loyalty? On the strength of those words I had put my life into his hands.

But if he meant what he said, how could he love Laure? I had enough sense left to know that I could not count on anyone.

3

Maria felt languid the next day, although her fever was down. When I offered to stay with her she insisted I go off to paint as usual; she was going to dress and come down and lie in the shade near the pool, and Egan would be with her whenever he could.

I went off and painted doggedly all day, as if I could erase from my mind what had happened. When I came down from the mountain in the evening I met Laure's car coming up from the main road. She stopped the car, braking so suddenly that the dust rose from under her wheels.

"Get in. You look hot and tired, *chérie*," she called out.

M. Abdykian was beside her. He moved over for me, making room, baring his square, too-even white teeth, enveloping me in a wave of heavy cologne that overcame even the smell of his cigar and the leather upholstery.

"Another painting?" he said. "You must show it to me. Perhaps I will buy it for my wife as a remembrance of La Ferme."

"I am sure Anna wants no remembrance of La Ferme," said Laure dryly. "It is bad enough that it takes up so much of your time."

"I always ask her to come with me," said Armad. "Why doesn't she come?"

"Because you are not very persuasive when you ask her, maybe," Laure said. "Why don't you stay at home with her?"

"You are in a dreadful temper," he said reproachfully.

"I come here for my nerves, but you make me even more nervous," she said. "I might as well stay at home."

"I am here only as a favor to your husband, you know that," said Armad.

"Pah," said Laure, and drew up with a wild sweep into the parking clearing.

Conor crossed from the shed to the kitchen door. He must have seen us, but he did not stop. It was Egan who came forward to take their bags. He was not smiling.

"An unexpected pleasure," he said, and kissed her cheek. "We did not expect you until tomorrow."

"I found myself in a dreadful state of nerves, darling," she said. "Nothing would do for me but La Ferme. Where is your brother?" Her voice was cold and flintlike.

"Where he always is. I'll tell him you're here."

I dreaded being with them that evening, and I was glad when Maria said she felt too tired for the dining room and would have dinner in her room. Now I had a reason to avoid the dining room myself. It began to rain early in the evening, so the terrace was deserted. I don't know where Laure and Armad were, presumably in the salon, but when I got ready for bed I noticed that the salon lights were out downstairs and most of the guests had used the rain as an excuse for getting to bed early. Were Laure and Conor alone together, or was there a council meeting among all of them, even Egan? No. I would have gambled anything on Conor not betraying me to them; he had been altogether too disturbed last night, altogether too concerned for my safety.

I was just as anxious to avoid Laure and Armad the next day, and took off even earlier than usual in the morning. La Ferme seemed tainted now, diseased beneath its ever more polished exterior. Maybe that was what drove me higher than ever before, out of sight of the last farm, the last rooftop.

I continued to climb until again, as I had found doing myself once before when I was too disturbed to paint, I reached a place on the mountainside where the soft green trees fell away and then the pines, and now the rock outcroppings were more evident. Far below and to my right I could see clear to the sea, and the town of Belan was a huddled cluster of dots of terra-cotta. There was no sound, only now and then a thin whistling of wind. I pulled on the thick red sweater I carried with me but seldom used. Now I made out the silver trickle of the river that ran beside La Ferme, as threadlike and shining as a snail's path. That speck of color must be the garden of the hotel; yes, there was the dark curl of the road between the trees. I wondered if they could see me from below. I was the only spot of color up here.

I don't know how long I stood there, fascinated by the vistas below me; the sun warmed me enough now to un-limber my cold fingers, and I stepped back from the edge and set my easel on a mossy level place. I sketched in the ravine below, and the few pines struggling out of the rock. It would be a canvas of pale grays and blues, a few accents of dark green, and the only other color the reddish veins in the rock. I worked steadily, only occasionally permitting my thoughts to stop me.

I was the best thing that had happened to him. How could he betray me to Armad? I sensed, no, I *knew* he would not let anyone hurt me. And, if he still loved Laure, he would never have said those words in the shed that night. I had always wondered about their relationship. I knew love was not rational, even inexplicable, and it was not hard to see why a woman as beautiful as Laure might have gotten under Conor's skin even if she were corrupt, and he knew it. I knew too that his reticence was part of him, and it was difficult for him to reveal his emotions, but still, to someone as eager as I to detect any clue to his feelings for her, why did I never feel some evidence of the attraction between them? Had it started as passion, and ended as business? Why did Armad spy on them in Conor's room?

I was hungry in spite of myself. My watch told me it was past one, and so I carried my lunch back to where there was a patch of grass and some scrubby pines that offered a little shade, and settling myself comfortably, I broke my cheese, and ate it with bites of crusty bread. There was a large sweet pear to finish it off, and then, warm, fed, I lay back and stared up at the cloudless sky until it began to tip dizzily, and then I shut my eyes.

I didn't sleep, only drowsed. There was a rustling somewhere below me, and I wondered if some farmer's goat or sheep had strayed this high. I had seen them before on the mountain, but they usually wore a bell tied with rope around their neck, and drowsily I wondered why I could not hear the dull metallic tinkling. It was too much of an effort to open my eyes; another five minutes, and then I must get back to work.

The rustling had stopped.

Suddenly, and for no reason, I felt uneasy. Not afraid, only that I had come very far from La Ferme, and there was no one within call. I had been in places as remote as this before without being afraid, but it was all the rest, I suppose, that colored my reaction. I felt as if someone were watching me. I told myself it was probably a goat. I tried to shake off the feeling by sitting up and getting back to work.

I was engulfed in blackness, furry and thick. It was in my nose and mouth, cutting off my breath, thick and black against my eyes. My scream was lost against the hand pressing the cloth to my mouth.

I was being dragged, my shoes catching on the rocks, an arm hard under my breasts. For a second I felt poised over nothing, a body heaving hard beside me as if to catch his breath, and then I was falling, falling, a terrible blow landing on my hip, my shoulder, rolling, falling, blows raining on my head, my arms, my legs— I knew nothing.

I opened my eyes, and was conscious only of pain. Blankly I saw the top of the mountain above me, stained red against a mauve sky. The mountain— I remembered. Someone had covered my face, and dragged me to the edge of the ravine and hurled me down.

At least my head wasn't so injured that I could not think. I put my hands to my face, and cried out, and my fingers came away stained brown. The cuts had almost dried. I moved a leg, an arm. I tried to sit up, but immediately began to roll down, sliding, bumping, crying out with pain as my body struck the hard earth. I could be grateful that here at least the naked rock was cushioned in earth and underbrush. I grasped blindly at whatever grew in my way, clutched and held onto a shrub, and arrested my fall.

I was alive. How, I could not imagine. I'd had the protection of a heavy sweater, its thick folded collar reaching my chin, but otherwise there was no reason why I should not have broken my neck.

I shuddered, not only from fear, but from the cold as well. The mountains cut the sun off early. I looked up at the sheer stone peaks, the warm color gone—

Something moved, dark against the sky, from the ledge where I had fallen.

Sheer terror stopped my breath, froze me motionless. My eyes teared and blurred against the sharp, pale light. A head peered over the edge, trying to find me. I blinked desperately, and looked again.

There was no one there.

Had I imagined it?

In the state of semishock I was in, it would be easy to imagine someone looking for me. I might even be hallucinating. And yet, if I had been pushed over, if someone had tried to kill me— *If* someone had tried to kill me? Could anything be more lightning clear in my mind than those last moments of terrifying helplessness when I was dragged inexorably toward the edge? But if someone had tried to kill me, would he not wait until he was sure he had succeeded? He might have thought me dead when I lay still, and then the sound of my second fall had shattered the silence, and brought him back.

I pressed into the shelter of the shrub. How long a time passed I don't know. I may even have lost consciousness. When I opened my eyes again the light was grayer, the cold more pronounced. I looked up and saw nobody. Far below me was the trickle of the Belan River, already lusterless in the dusk, almost indetectable except for the outline of trees that bordered its banks. I had to get down to the river. Belan lay there, and La Ferme.

And what awaited me at La Ferme? A murderer? I should get to the police at Belan first . . . *Maria was at La Ferme. I had to get back to her.* The murderer had not dared attack there before. I must get to her as fast as I could, and we must leave there, tonight if possible.

Desperately I tried to stand upright, and fell. The ground was too steep, my legs too weak. I half-sat up and controlling my descent that way I slid and bumped down, clutching at whatever lay near, a rock, or a bush, or a tree trunk. Now and then I had to stop. The pain in my bruised, sore body was enough to make me sob out loud in spite of my efforts to make no sound.

Pebbles skittered above me.

They were too high up for me to have disturbed them. Someone else was there, someone following me.

My heart began to hammer. My mind went blank with fear. I had to think clearly, I must. My life depended on it.

He cannot be sure I know he is there. He will think that I will continue my way down toward the river.

I glanced around me. The trees and bushes grew more and more dense, providing more cover the lower I went. But for him as well as me. And he was not exhausted, his senses were keener. My eyes darted frantically ahead, trying to plan a way I might proceed. I must not drop down directly to the river as I had been doing. He would expect that. Rather I would encircle the mountain on the line I was now until I was directly above La Ferme, and only then risk the descent.

I must make no sound. Moving with infinite care, I crept toward the shelter of the next bush, then the next. When I tried to stand upright I almost cried out; I must have sprained my leg. Trembling, rubbing my leg, I leaned against a tree trunk to rest.

It was growing darker, which would help me. And *him*. A wind blew up as it often did in the evening, which would muffle the sound of my movements. And *his*. Despair enveloped me. Someone had tried to kill me. *Someone had tried to kill me.* It was a bad dream. It could not be happening to me.

A branch snapped.

I heard it distinctly. Where? My senses had grown dull. Above me? To the side from which I'd come? Close? Far away? I listened with dreadful concentration, but there was no more sound. He was cunning, he would not give himself away again.

I moved with laborious caution.

It must be eight o'clock. My watch had stopped at two, when I was attacked. They must be looking for me at La Ferme. Maria would insist they call the police. Unless they had done something to her, too.

Fright and anger and frustration drove me on.

The murderer would join in the search for me. If he didn't, he would give himself away. If I managed to get back alive, he would even pretend great relief and happiness that I was found.

If I was found. My mind was wandering. I remembered trip through the Gorges of the Tarn with my parents wh was a little girl, and the driver of the car pointing out a bus and all its passengers had fallen to the bottom of ravine and lain there undetected for hours. And that had been the Gorges of the Tarn, where tourist buses go all the time. Who came to the ravine of the little Belan River? There wasn't even a road. I remembered a story of a murderer who had buried the body of his victim beneath the leaves of a tree in the forest, and she had been found only in winter when all the leaves had been blown away.

Far below me I saw faint lights. La Ferme! I wept, I think, and wiped tears and perspiration from my face with the sleeve of my sweater. I must start down.

But first I listened. The wind was stronger here, funneling through the mountains, and I could hear nothing. It was pitch black. He might have lost me. I dared not take off my red sweater, which might still give off a glimmer of color to my pursuer. Without it I might freeze. The murderer might have counted on that. Even if I had not been killed instantly I might have broken some bones so I could not move, and would have died on the mountainside from cold and exhaustion.

He might be waiting below. He might guess that I would have to come out here sooner or later. The ground was less precipitous now, the slope more gradual; the trees were thinner and goats had nibbled away at the brush, and I would be more visible. At least the darkness was complete, with only the thinnest fraction of a moon. I could hear the sound of the river below.

I began to inch my way down.

Please let it not be Conor who tried to kill me. Let it not be Egan, either, for Maria's sake. But it could be either, because of the heroin. *If* they were shipping heroin. I could not imagine either of them a murderer. Can you fall in love with a murderer? Who else could it be? I am too trustful. My friends in grade school would ask me scornfully, "Do you

believe everything people tell you?" You are the best thing
that ever happened to me. Suppose I endanger his life, and
his brother's? Whose life is more important?

I caught my breath. Ahead of me a strong beam of light
played on the river.

It was a floodlight. It must be people searching for me.
The police. Cry out! Run!

My reactions were slow because of pain and exhaustion.
The light played along the river. They must think I have
drowned. It skimmed up on both banks—

A man's head and shoulders were silhouetted against the
floodlight. For an instant only, just below me, toward the
river; the light moved on, the head vanished into blackness.

A cry rose and stayed dumb in my throat. I stood motionless until my heart beat less furiously. To reach the river I
would have to pass my pursuer so closely that he could seize
me and stifle my shouts long before anyone could reach me.
Whichever way I moved, he would hear me, he was too close.
I was trapped here. In moments the floodlight would move
away, with the searchers, and I would be left alone with the
murderer. Lie quiet? Outwait him? It was my only chance.

I must have been out of my mind. Hardly aware of the
pain in my leg, I began to run with a sudden desperate spurt
of energy. Someone's voice rang in my ears—mine?—high and
hoarse in the stillness: "Here! Here!"

The floodlight seemed to tremble, hesitating, darting aim-
lessly; it came toward me. I ran into its embracing, protective
circle. Water splashed to my knees. I was in the river.

"Here! Here!"

My eyes were dazzled. Voices grew louder around me;
there was the insistent blowing of a car horn, picked up by

another. The rustle and splashing grew. I was surrounded.

They had a kind of canvas into which they lifted me, covering me with a blanket, carrying me up the steep slope to the dirt path where cars clustered. My eyes blinked in the headlights; questions rang in my ears. Egan bent over me.

"Thank God you're all right."

Where was Conor? They talked of the hospital. "No! I want to go home!" Maria was at La Ferme. I had to get to her.

Other voices, urging me, even Egan's: "The hospital would be the best place—"

"I'm all right! I want to go home!"

Then I saw Conor's face, his hair blazing like a disordered golden crest in the light of the headlamps.

"We'll take her to La Ferme," he said. "We can put her on the back seat. Egan, you go ahead and tell Maria she's all right."

Then Maria must still be safe. I fell back, and let Conor's and other hands lift me to the back seat of the Citroën. I cried out in pain, and they doubled a blanket under my sprained leg.

Conor touched my leg. "I don't think it's broken—"

I turned my face away from him. "Just take me home."

It was only minutes to La Ferme, but they drove slowly to spare me the jolting. Maria was on the steps when I drove up. Her face was strained and she had been crying, but she tried to laugh.

"Falling down a mountain, Carrie! Couldn't you find someplace safer to paint?

With Conor she helped me undress and get into bed. Camille brought me hot tea laced with brandy, and Maria fed it to me by spoonfuls. I dozed now and then from exhaustion, but I could hear their low voices, Conor's and Egan's and Maria's.

Dr. Froissart arrived and examined me thoroughly. He touched my leg and I winced, and he said, "Tomorrow if you cannot walk on it perhaps you will come to Digne where it can be X-rayed, yes? For possible fracture. Meanwhile, we can make you more comfortable."

He sponged down my bruises with soap and warm water and alcohol, and he cleaned the deep cut on my forehead and brought the edges together with tape. He gave me an injection for the pain, and told me I was a lucky girl that I was alive, and then he told everyone to leave me and let me sleep, which was what I needed most.

Dr. Froissart's injection was already taking effect. I managed to murmur my thanks to him, and my good-nights to the others, and lapsed into sleep almost at once.

I don't know how much later it was, maybe only minutes, when I opened my eyes with a start, my heart beating hard. I was dazed and drugged, and had been dreaming grotesque dreams, and as my blurred eyes tried to focus I saw a thin crack of light around my door.

It widened, my door was opening.

I tried to sit up and cry out, but the drug was too powerful, like lead in my veins.

It was Conor, large and looming closer. He bent over me.

"What do you want?" I tried to say, but the syllables ran together thickly.

"Go to sleep," he said.

"No, no—"

I must have tried to rise, but his hands put me back on the

pillow. Dully I watched while he pushed my chair in front of
the door and sat down in it.

I was trapped there.

Call out, my mind told me. Someone will hear you. But I
couldn't even keep my eyes open. I slept again, and when I
woke it was noon, and he was gone, and my chair was back in
its place, so maybe I dreamed it all.

4

Maria must have been hovering close all morning, because
when I returned from the bathroom on stiff, sore legs which
nevertheless supported me, she was waiting in my room.

"How do you feel? Should you be up? What a scare you
gave us, Carrie!"

"I'll live, I guess. I'm sorry about scaring you."

I sounded grumpy. A look in the bathroom mirror had
almost made me turn tail and run and hide. Not only the
patch on my forehead and the cuts too small to cover, my hair
was a tangle, and my eyes were hollow, and besides, my head
ached, and the rest of me hurt. I should have been grateful
that nothing was broken, but now I had other equally pain-
ful facts to face.

"Let me bring you some breakfast. Or brunch. Soup? That
should be good for you."

She ran downstairs, and I got into bed again, shakier than I
had thought I'd be. We must get out, and fast, before another
attempt was made on my life. And maybe this time on Maria's. Could I drive? I couldn't, as I felt now, but Maria
could, at least as far as Nice, where we could leave the car and
get a plane to Paris.

The important thing was, how to make Maria come? The

only way would be to tell her what had happened on the mountain, and about the heroin. But could I depend on her reaction? Might she not still tell Egan? How could I be sure that Egan had not been involved in the attempt to kill me? There was that very real possibility that Conor had told Egan about my discovery in the picture frames, and— But did I have to go through that whole train of futile conjecture again? Whoever it was, it no longer mattered. We must get away, and at once.

There was a tap on the door. I thought it was Maria, and I said, "Come in."

It was Conor.

"How are you feeling?"

The female in me was still uppermost, even though I might be confronting my murderer. I turned my bruised face into the pillow.

"Better, thanks."

He said, "That was a stupid thing to do, poise yourself on the edge of a ravine."

I forgot my face.

"I was not on the edge of the ravine."

His face reflected nothing.

"How did it happen, then?"

"I was thrown down."

"Come now, Carrie."

"I'm not that stupid that I don't know when my face is covered by someone who doesn't want me to see who he is and I am dragged several yards to the edge and pushed over."

He did look sick.

I went on bitterly, to say out loud another thought I had brooded on during last night's dreadful march along the bottom of the ravine, "And I think Mlle. Sophie was pushed out of her window in the same way. By someone who thought she knew too much.''

He did not deny it, only continued to stand there, the sick look deepening in his eyes and around his mouth.

''I suppose you will tell me now to keep these theories to myself, for my own good. But whom am I really protecting, Conor?''

He walked out.

Maria came in almost at once, with Egan carrying my breakfast tray.

''Maria says you're good as new. What about those X rays?'' he said, settling the tray on my lap. ''I think they'd be a good idea, just in case.''

''I'm sure I don't—'' And then I thought, it will be a way to get Maria out of the house, where we can talk, and to Digne, where I can phone Nice and make the plane reservations without being overheard and my plan stirring the murderer into action. ''Well, maybe I should,'' I said slowly. ''Maria, could you drive me?''

''I'll drive you, of course,'' Egan said.

''I don't want to take you away from La Ferme, not with so many people here.''

The corridor had been busy with early arrivals. I could hear them from my room.

''I can manage—''

''So can Maria and I,'' I said, more firmly than was natural. I thought he looked at me oddly, but then he and Maria exchanged glances, and he shrugged.

''Of course, if you prefer,'' he said, and left us.

Maria looked at me. ''What was that all about?''

''I choose to go alone with you. Do you mind?''

''No,'' she said slowly. ''Only—''

"Would you call Dr. Froissart, and tell him we're coming?"

While she went downstairs to the telephone, I managed to pull on my clothes, and comb my hair in such a way that it fell over the tape on my forehead. I could not even try to disguise the cuts with powder, and let them alone. As I dressed, I took mouthfuls of the food on my tray. I was too distraught to eat, thinking of the look on Conor's face. My story could have been a surprise to him. That drawn, haggard look could have been shock, and even fear for me. I wanted to believe that. Then, why hadn't he said something, asked me more questions, discussed what to do, called in the police? But he'd walked away as if to terminate the issue, as if he didn't want to hear any more.

Maria brought the car around to the porch, and I let myself down gingerly, and got in. I pleaded soreness, and made her drive slowly. Not until the road straightened out on the last five miles before Digne did I talk to her about my plans. I hoped to get away without divulging too much; I hoped she would accede, because of my accident.

"I want to go home, at once, Maria. I'd like to reserve seats from Nice for tomorrow."

Her face went blank. Surprise? Resistance? But she didn't say anything.

"I know how you feel about Egan, about leaving him, but it's August already, and he plans to be in New York in the fall, so you won't miss too much time together."

She let her breath out in almost a sigh.

"Maria, I've lost heart in La Ferme, somehow. I wouldn't ask you to leave now if I didn't feel I couldn't stick it out here any longer."

"Just because you had an accident, Carrie?" And then she added hurriedly, "I'm not making it out to be nothing. It was

simply awful for you, and you might have been killed, but
. . . but you can get better here as well as at home."

"There was Mlle. Sophie's fall," I said. I didn't even want
to say as much as that, I didn't want her to guess my suspicions.

She turned her head. I had the feeling suddenly that she
already knew my suspicions, but was stubbornly resisting
them.

"She was lightheaded and weak, she slipped— You mustn't
brood over it."

"I'm not brooding," I said. "I just don't like the pattern,
even if they're accidents. That razor— That wasn't an accident."

I don't know why the memory of that first night I met Miss
Waldron should have come back to me, the man on the sidewalk, the stolen package; it was as if a pattern of violence had
followed us here.

She tried to laugh. "It's not like you to be so jittery."

"Maria," I said with a show of firmness, "I'm reserving two
seats on the plane tomorrow. I expect you to come with me. I
wouldn't insist if I didn't think it was important."

She started to say something but apparently changed her
mind. The stubborn look remained on her face, however,
and I wondered if I had enough influence to make her do
what I asked. What was my choice if she didn't? Tell her the
whole story, including the heroin. And if she still refused? I
couldn't with any conscience leave her here alone, and as a
last resort I might have to go to the police.

Dr. Froissart X-rayed my leg from hip to toe, and then had
us wait in the office while he developed the prints enough so
that he could read them. It gave me the chance to make my
phone call. Ostentatiously I went over to the nurse and asked

her if there was a telephone here that I might use; the charge would be added to my bill. She gestured toward a small consulting room, and offered to put the call through for me. Maria was watching, but she said nothing, not even when the nurse repeated the call I had asked her to make: "The Nice International Airport, yes?"

The call went through, and I was able to have them hold space for us on the nine o'clock flight to Paris. We would have to be at the ticket desk by eight o'clock to claim our seats.

"They're holding two tickets for us for tomorrow night."

She set her chin; I knew she would not come along docilely.

The X rays showed no fracture or damage of any kind, but then I had been sure that they wouldn't. My purpose had been accomplished. When we got back in the car I said, "Would it be too much to ask you to keep our leaving a secret?"

"Not even tell Egan?" she said incredulously.

I nodded.

"But why?"

"If it weren't terribly important, Maria, I wouldn't ask you."

"I think that fall affected your brain or something," she said. "Is this all supposed to get back at Conor because he's still in love with Laure?"

"Do you want me to answer that seriously?"

"But really, Carrie, if I'm to treat Egan so *awfully*, not to even tell him that we're going until the last minute, I should know why."

"I'll tell you why. On the plane."

The car shuddered, and faltered, as she changed gear.

We drove into La Ferme at dusk. The dining room was crowded. I felt very tired, and gave the accident as an excuse to ask for my dinner in bed. Maria was angry, or unwilling to talk, and only came in briefly to wish me a sullen good-night. I had no way of knowing if she had confided our plans to Egan or not. In any case, I locked my door.

Camille knocked, with a pot of hot tea to help me sleep.

I asked her, "When did Mme. Patrelcis and M. Abdykian leave that day of my fall?"

"But as usual," she said, surprised at my question. "They had breakfast late, and stayed to swim in the pool, and then they left. I did not notice the time precisely."

It did not matter. If they had really wanted to find me, there would have been time for Armad to leave Laure in the car and follow me on foot.

It was just that I wanted so desperately to believe it was Armad, rather than Conor or Egan. What reason could Armad have, unless Conor had told him about the heroin, and they were all in it together? If Conor had told him, then . . . then he had wanted me killed.

A weight pressed on my chest, stifling my breath. I couldn't even answer that tentative knock on my door. The second knock was louder.

"Who is it?"

"Conor."

I hesitated.

"I just wanted to return your painting things."

I felt so much despair that I almost did not care what danger I might be in. I put on a robe and opened the door for him.

He put my paints and folded easel on a chair.

I said, tightly, "How did you know where to find them?"

He didn't notice anything in my question. "I went up the mountain. I spent the good part of the afternoon looking."

"Thanks for finding them."

He said, "You were too damn close to the edge, you know."

"I wasn't that close," I said. "I'm not an idiot. I made a point of setting up the easel a good distance back from the edge."

"I suppose someone moved it after you fell."

"Why not?" I said. "If someone were trying to hide the fact that my fall was no accident."

"*If* someone were trying to hide it. You seem so damn sure someone was trying to kill you. Isn't it possible that you were scared, and justifiably, after finding the heroin, and that you were ready to believe someone was after you?"

"Do you think I only imagined that cloth over my face?"

He doggedly ignored my scorn. "People in a certain state of mind can imagine anything. Your fall shocked you. It could have confused your thinking."

"As a matter of fact, I'd taken my lunch and eaten it a good distance back from where I'd been painting," I said. "The man who attacked me had to drag me to the edge."

"You'd just eaten your lunch? You could have been sleepy. Dazed by the sun. You might have staggered when you stood up—"

For an instant I was shaken. I *had* been afraid. I might have been half asleep, and lost my balance. I remembered the horror of suffocating blackness, someone's sweater pushed over my face, my heels catching on the rocks. No, I couldn't have imagined it!

"Wait a second!" I ran to the closet and found the shoes I'd worn that day. All the color had been scuffed off the backs from having been dragged. "Look at the marks!"

He said, "You could have done that in falling."

"Why are you determined to make me believe it was an accident?" I said evenly.

He stared at me, hard pressed. He said, "If someone tried to kill you, why shouldn't he try again?"

I met his eyes. "I've thought of that."

"You shouldn't be alone," he said. "I'll stay here with you."

I said, still evenly, "I'd rather be alone. I'll keep my door locked."

He flushed darkly. Without another word he turned and let himself out. I pointedly locked my door while he was still within earshot.

VI

❧

❧

❧

1

I PLANNED TO PUT OFF PACKING as late as possible so that no hint of our intention could possibly leak out. Pleading exhaustion, though I was remarkably recovered, I spent the morning reading in a chaise beside the pool. That was how I saw Laure when she arrived.

I was surprised to see her. She peered around, looking for Conor, no doubt, but he was not in sight this morning. She seemed less carefully groomed than usual. Her hair especially seemed almost unkempt, and she was wearing something green which emphasized the sallowness of her skin. She never came back after such a short interval. Today was Thursday, and she had left only Tuesday, the day of my accident—it seemed simpler to call it that. Besides, she made a point of being at the villa in Cannes on the weekends, when her husband returned. And where was Armad?

I waved to her, and she came toward me, making an obvious effort to compose her face.

"I see you are better. I am glad for you, *chérie*. Conor told me you'd had a bad fall. Where is everyone?"

"They're around somewhere. I haven't seen anybody."

"I will put on a swimsuit and join you."

It took her a while to return, so I presumed she had found Conor. She wore a shred of fabric over her breasts and hips, and her figure though full was smooth and flawless. Drawing a chaise over to where I lay, she flung herself into it, and then turned her head to study my cuts with cool interest.

"They will heal," she said. "You are very lucky." But she was too impatient to maintain even a polite interest in me. "Now that they are doing so well with the hotel, you would think they would have someone at the pool to take the orders for the bar."

"Jeanne is here after lunch. They haven't much call this early."

"I'll find her." She got up and went to the house, returning in a short while with Camille trailing her, carrying a small round tray with whiskey and a bottle of Perrière. "Come back in a little while again," she called after Camille.

She finished her whiskey in two gulps. She was plainly not herself. I could see hollows and shadows on her face that I had never seen before.

"Aren't you well, Laure?"

She expelled cigarette smoke between her teeth.

"I should not be here. I told no one, not even Armad."

"You must have had a good reason to come."

Her glance swept me with veiled scorn. "Even if I did, I should not have come alone. I promised my husband I would always take Armad and Anna, or at least Armad, with me."

"Then why didn't you?"

Her mouth tightened. "Because I cannot bear him."

"If you tell your husband that you don't like M. Abdy-kian's company, won't he understand?"

"He would be offended," she said. "Armad is a cousin, someone my husband trusts. And not only would I offend him, but Sarif would become suspicious, and would wonder if perhaps there was a reason why I preferred to come alone."

"But all last year you came alone," I said.

"And how long would he continue to believe that I came for my nerves?" she said. Her laugh was contemptuous. "My husband is not stupid. For a while perhaps I could make him believe that I had found a delightful new place that was good for me. But by now I should have been bored. My husband knows there are other places, nearer, and infinitely better. Armad would have told him that. He must have begun to wonder for some time, otherwise I would not have had to travel with a man of my family, like a good Turkish wife."

She laughed with bitterness. "You and Armad have something in common."

"I'm not here to watch Maria," I said.

"Perhaps she needs someone who would."

"I thought you were French, not Turkish," I said.

"Even so. If she were my child I would want her on her guard against a man like Egan. He has been spoiled by too many women."

"She is old enough to learn how to deal with him herself," I said. "She knows him better than either of us."

She shrugged.

"Perhaps you are right. She will not be the first seventeen-year-old to have her heart broken. Besides, her fortune will buy her all the handsome men she wants." She shrugged again. "I cannot imagine anyone who needs our sympathy less, yes?"

Camille arrived with her second drink. "Luncheon is served."

Laure said, "Let us have lunch together. Please. I do not want to be alone."

I waited for her to finish her drink. She rose, and fastened a long skirt over her, and we went to the hotel. When I peered into the dining room Maria was not there.

"Let me see if Maria wants her lunch now," I said. "You go ahead. I'll join you in a moment."

I knocked on Maria's door.

"Come in."

She was dressed to go out. "I'm driving to Digne with Egan. He has to order wine."

"I thought he just did."

"You know they only order in small quantities. They can't afford to stock up," she said shortly. Plainly, she was still irritated with me.

"Are you having lunch?"

"I had mine before."

"Maria, you know we should leave no later than six. Maybe five thirty. I don't know the road to Nice as well as Egan, and I can't drive as fast."

"I know."

"Have you said anything to Egan?"

"Stop hounding me, Carrie. I told you I wouldn't."

There was nothing I could say, no argument with which I could appease her. All I wanted now was for her to come to Nice with me tonight even if she never spoke to me again. I went back to the dining room and joined Laure at her table.

"Where is Maria? Is everybody in hiding?" she said fretfully.

"Maria is driving to Digne with Egan. He has some shopping to do."

She filled her wineglass, and then remembered her manners. "Carrie?"

I shook my head. "I'm not used to wine at lunch yet."

Her elbow struck the wine bottle and knocked it over. Wine spread in a red stain over the cloth. She stared at it in horror. "My God!"

"It's nothing," I said, picking up the bottle, and unfolding my napkin over the stain. "Laure, don't you have a pill of some kind, a tranquilizer?" I found myself pitying her. That smooth-as-cream exterior was sagging, fading.

She shook her head. "I am afraid of drugs."

I thought. "Why don't you call Armad?" I said. "Tell him you're feeling ill, that you came here on the spur of the moment. Tell him you didn't want to interrupt him at work to tell him you were coming here, and that you'll be home by evening."

"How can I drive home tonight?"

"Conor could drive you."

Her glance said I was a fool. "I would not want my husband to know he had driven me home."

"But you're ill."

She shrugged. "Do you think that would make any difference?"

I watched her drink too much wine, and wondered if I should try and find Conor.

"My husband does not like me to come here," she said. "I don't know what Armad said to him, but Sarif would like me to go elsewhere to rest. When he phoned me from Istanbul he was very explicit. He does not order me, you understand, he knows I am French, but he spoke to me very strongly. I would prefer that you not go to La Ferme anymore, you understand me, Laure, he said. Very explicit. And here I am, at La Ferme."

Her breath came in a sob.

"Why don't you go up to your room and rest now?" I said. "And then when you wake up maybe you will feel well enough to drive home before your husband returns. Maybe no one will even have to know you were here. You can say you went somewhere. Visiting. Sight-seeing."

"Yes. Yes," she mumbled, her eyes puffy, her face stained with an unbecoming color.

She let me help her upstairs, turn down her bed, and darken the room. I went into my own room and locked the door. No one would need to come in now; Jeanne had put the room in order, and did not have to return until dinner when she would turn down the beds, a refinement which Egan had added now that there was more help. I could safely pack, and if Jeanne were to notice that my clothes were no longer in the armoire, Maria and I would be safely on our way by then.

I took out my suitcase and packed carefully, deliberately wasting time. I had over two hours to spend until Maria and I left, and nothing to do. I didn't dare risk bringing my valise and painting gear to the car, for fear of meeting Conor. Better to appear on the terrace just at the moment of departure, all our baggage with us. The terrace would be crowded by then, and whoever wanted to see me dead would have no time to make any plans. He could only stand by helplessly while we loaded the Citroën and drove away.

I sank across my bed, engulfed suddenly with thoughts of

that sterile, desolate room in New York to which I was returning. *If* you make it back alive, I told myself. The menace of
La Ferme will be three thousand miles away; at least you'll
be safe. Conor, too, would be three thousand miles away. I
will never see him again. And suppose he tried to kill you
back there on the mountain, would you still regret him? You
are weird, I told myself, echoing Maria's words. Even if he is
not a murderer, he may be protecting the murderer. Even if
he is not engaged in the traffic of drugs, he is plainly protecting someone who is. Even if it is someone he loves, he
weighed that life against yours. If there is anything more
loathsome than cold-blooded murder, it is the murder of
many, through the sale of drugs. When you do fall in love, I
told myself in despair, you do one fine job of it.

Imagine Maria's state of mind, if she were to suspect Egan.

Maria? Was she going to be late? I'd heard no sound
from her room. Surely she would have let me know, if she
had come back, even if she was angry with me. I went to
her room and tapped on the door. No answer. I turned the
doorknob, and the door opened. I looked in. The room was
empty.

It was in the same disorder as when I'd seen it at lunchtime. Discarded jeans on the bed, a bathing suit hanging
from a doorknob, a plate with a half-eaten peach and the
peach pit of a second on the bureau beside a tangle of silk
scarfs.

Damn. I went back to my room and put on the cotton dress
I would travel in, put my valise in the armoire and my large
handbag and raincoat beside it, and went downstairs to sit on
the terrace and wait for her. We could still get on the plane if
we were late, and there were seats available, and even if we

couldn't, we would be gone from here, and could take a room in Nice and wait for the morning plane.

Camille brought me my usual vermouth on ice.

"M. Egan not back yet?" I asked her casually.

She shook her head.

A half hour went by, and then an hour. Camille came out to me. "Would you like to dine on the terrace?"

"Thanks, Camille. I'm not hungry. I'd like to wait for Maria."

"You are worried? But you must not. They are enjoying themselves somewhere together, you understand."

I understood.

It was seven, it was seven thirty. We could not possibly make the plane anymore. And that was why she hadn't troubled to remonstrate too much, or to tell Egan. She had simply arranged it that she wouldn't be on the plane, and maybe she hoped that I might go alone. I couldn't go alone.

Conor came out on the terrace. It was rare to see him there this early, when guests were being served their coffee. He came up to me.

"Camille says you're not having your dinner."

"I'm waiting for Maria. She isn't back yet."

"They went to Digne, she and Egan."

"I know. But it never takes them this long."

"They might have stayed out for the evening. They often do."

"She wouldn't, tonight. She—" I stopped. He was looking at me curiously. I flushed. I said, "She would have told me."

"She's safe, with Egan," he said.

"Can you guarantee that?"

"Would you take my word, if I said I could?"

I couldn't lie. I turned away.

"I suggest you have your dinner."

"I couldn't eat," I muttered. "I think we should call the police."

"What would we tell them, that a young man and woman who went out together are a few hours late coming home?"

"There might have been an accident." I couldn't tell him why I was so disturbed, I couldn't give away our plans.

"If the police had heard about an accident, we'd have known too, by now." He looked at me. "But I'll phone, if you want."

I followed him to the telephone in the hall. Let him know that I do not trust him, it no longer mattered. I watched him as he asked for the number, and heard the crackling response at the other end. I could even make out some of the words, so I knew he was speaking to the police. No, there were no accidents reported between here and Digne. They would have to check the other districts, they would call back if they heard anything. Yes, they had a record of those admitted to the hospital of the region, no, there was no one by the names we had given.

He put down the phone.

"Where could they be?" I asked, my voice thin.

"Where could who be?"

I looked up to see Laure on the stairs. She had put on one of her flowered chiffon pajamas, and drawn her hair back, so that she looked more her usual self, but there were dark circles under her eyes that emphasized her pallor.

"Maria hasn't come back."

She lifted her eyebrows. "Wasn't she with Egan?"

"Neither of them is back."

She laughed. "But how amusing, for them."

"The dining room will be closing soon, Laure," Conor said. "Why don't you go in and have your dinner."

"Ah, but *le patron* would always see to it that the dining room was open for me, is that not so, Conor?"

"You know it is," he said evenly. "But it would make it simpler for the women if you ate now."

"You are both so worried!" she said, looking from one to the other of us. "What great harm can be done? Is it that you feel you have been negligent, my dear Carrie? But you should have known this would happen, and has happened before. After all, why is she here, so far from home, in this dreary place!"

"Coming, Laure?" said Conor, from the doorway.

"I am coming, darling," she said, laughing again.

I went back to the terrace and sat where I could watch the gate. She must have known that I would not leave if it were this late. Even if I had made a remarkable recovery, I was still not strong enough to drive for several hours along those mountain roads at night. If Maria had stayed away to keep us from leaving tonight, why didn't she return now? She had accomplished her purpose. Unless she had let slip to Egan what my intention was, and it was Egan who had taken her away, it was Egan who intended to keep her out of reach.

Laure joined me, carrying her brandy glass.

"Still not back. Ah, well, it means nothing."

Not to you.

Her breath was sour with wine. "But you are acting as if it were some great tragedy, Carrie dear! They will be back, once they are bored with their adventure."

"I wonder if they've eloped," I said. I was too agitated to

keep the idea to myself, but she was too drunk to pay it any serious attention.

"You are naïve, *chérie*."

"Is it so impossible? They're in love."

She laughed. "*She* is in love."

"Why do you think he isn't?" I said evenly.

"I know his kind of man. He is a professional. When her letter came he told us, Conor and me, what a bore it was, her coming for the summer. But she was a very pretty and very rich bore, and the summers are so dull here anyway, so it would not be too bad, all in all."

I stared at her, speechless. She was quite drunk, and might not know what she was saying. Still, she was too drunk to invent a story. So Miss Waldron was to have her worst fears confirmed.

Only . . . only why didn't I believe Laure? I couldn't put out of my mind the image of their meeting that night we came. I couldn't put out of my mind the way he looked at her, talked to her. He had to love her, he had to. How could I be so wrong?

You fell in love with Conor, didn't you?

At midnight Conor and I helped Laure to her room. I left him with her, and went to my own room and locked the door. I was so exhausted that I even slept.

2

I overslept, as if my body had insisted it take the rest it needed in spite of me. Dazedly I saw the sun in my room with the sharp clarity of midday; it was hot, and my skin was damp

with perspiration. Maria! I remembered, and got out of bed
as hastily as I could with my sore leg, washed and dressed and
hurried to her room.

"Maria?"

No answer. I turned the knob. The room had been ordered, the clothes hung away, the half-eaten peach gone. She
might have slept there, and left, but the room had the curious emptiness of one that had not been lived in for a time.

Someone was hammering. It had to be Conor. I traced him
to one of the new bathrooms, where he was trying to get a
shower to work.

"They haven't come back." It wasn't even a question.

He shook his head briefly.

"Shouldn't you call the police again?"

"I have. There's nothing new."

"Could we take the car and drive along the road to Digne?
Maybe they've had an accident but they haven't been found."

"The road to Digne is fairly straight below Belan. No precipices. No ravines. It's relatively well traveled. If they'd had
an accident they would have been seen."

I stared at him, as if I could see in his face what he was
thinking. He was concerned, I could see that, but beyond,
nothing. He was frowning over the shower head, turning it
in his strong fingers, his eyes intent on the job he was doing.
As I watched him it seemed ludicrous, absurd, that he could
be a part of this business going on under cover of the hotel.
But I had been fooled too often by his look of honesty; I
would not let myself be fooled again.

He looked up and caught me off guard, and misunderstood
what must have been my frown.

He said, "Did you tell Maria about the heroin?"

"I didn't. Did you think that might have something to do with their disappearance?"

"I'm only speculating. Like you," he said grimly, stopping to mop up some spilled water with a discarded bath towel, tossing it into a corner.

I followed him out into the hall. I said in a low voice, "You're Egan's brother. You know him well enough to have some idea of where he might go, what he might do."

"You know Maria. Does that give *you* any clues?"

"I think she would follow him blindly. And refuse him nothing."

"If it's sex you're thinking of, they can have it here."

"I wasn't only thinking of sex. He might have reasons of his own for wanting to keep her away."

"You think he kidnapped her?" he said ironically.

"You know something!" I cried. "You've always known something that you're hiding about Egan!"

"He'll never harm Maria," he said.

"Maybe Armad—"

But he turned away abruptly. "I don't know Armad."

Plainly, he didn't want to talk about Armad.

I went downstairs and had my breakfast, even though the early arrivals among the guests were already lunching on the terrace, under the umbrellas, flowered, that had just made their appearance at La Ferme. The heat was scorching, the air breathless, and I hurried to the shade at the far side of the pool as soon as I had finished. Laure found me there.

"Laure! I thought you would be gone by now!"

"I am too distraught to drive."

"Have you spoken to Conor about taking you home?"

"Even if I were to chance that, Conor would not want to

leave while Egan and his little friend are away amusing themselves."

I myself preferred Conor to stay here until we heard some news.

"But what about your husband? Won't he be home today?"

"I am not well enough to travel," she said, sullenly.

"Should you call Armad?"

"I don't want him here."

"Maybe you could leave a message for your husband to come and fetch you."

"He would never make this drive. He detests driving even on good roads. And especially now, that I have come here against his express wishes. Perhaps he will not want me to come home."

"He could send Armad for you," I said, ignoring her last statement, dismissing it as melodrama.

"Armad drives horribly," she said. "Please, *please*, let us not talk about it anymore. I cannot think!"

She stood up abruptly, flung off her robe, and dived into the pool; her blond head emerged, darkened and streaming, and she began to plow with strong white arms through the water.

Camille stood above, near the hedge. "Mlle. Belding. The telephone."

Maria. It had to be about Maria. I jumped up and began to run, ignoring the soreness in my leg. I seized the telephone just as Conor came into the entry. Camille must have called him, too.

"Carrie?"

"Maria!" I almost broke down in my relief. "Where are you?"

"I'm in Marseilles. We'll be back by dinner."

"Marseilles!" I looked at Conor. "They're all right! They're in Marseilles!" I turned back to the phone. "You *are* all right?"

"I'm all right. I'm disappointed, that's all," she said in a thin voice. "I thought we'd come back married, but I'm still Maria Waldron. Don't ask me any questions," she said, her voice even thinner as if it might break completely. "I'll tell you when I get back."

She hung up. I turned, hardly aware of Laure standing dripping on the stones of the entry. I said, "They went to get married."

"To get married!" he repeated.

"Are they married?" Laure said.

I shook my head. "She said she'd tell me about it when they got back."

"So. All the fuss and worry, and for nothing," Laure said. Her mouth, loose from so much drinking, twisted into a grimace. "Perhaps that silly child will have learned something, at least."

Conor was watching her. And then, unpredictably, he went to her and put his arm around her and walked her away. I had never seen them embrace. Something caught in my throat.

Egan and Maria returned after dinner, timing their entrance for when the terrace would be crowded with diners and they could expect little attention. They waved at me, and said they were going into the kitchen for something to eat.

I gave them a chance to finish their meal, and when I saw them carry their coffee into the salon I joined them. Conor wasn't around; I asked them if they'd seen him.

"Just in passing," Egan said. He looked more tense than his casual manner suggested.

"Whatever you do, don't blame Egan," Maria said. "It was my fault." Her voice was thick, as if she had been crying.

"It was my fault as much as yours," Egan said. "Don't imply that it was all your suggestion that we get married."

"It was my idea that we get married *now,*" she said. "You know you would have preferred to wait. But Carrie was going to make me go home last night and so—"

She stopped, and darted a glance at me. She had given me away. Egan's eyes narrowed.

He said, "Make you go home?" He looked at me. "Did you plan on going back to the States last night, Carrie?"

"I—" How could I answer him? "I felt . . . mixed up—After that fall I had, I . . . just felt I wanted to go home."

He was looking at Maria now. "Why didn't you say something about this to me?"

"I couldn't. I promised Carrie."

"I see."

"But you don't see, you don't at all!" she cried. "I would never have kept it from you if it hadn't been so important to Carrie! I don't even know why it was! She seemed to think so!"

"Then maybe you'll tell me, Carrie, why you had to keep your plans secret."

My mind would not come up with an answer. I floundered miserably with some inept reasons, but luckily for me Conor came in just then, angrier than I had ever seen him.

"What the devil was this all about?"

"I don't think it's any of your business," Egan said.

"You had us worried. Doesn't that make it our business?"

"I'm sorry you worried. Getting married was a private decision." He spoke evenly now. "We had hoped to be able to keep it secret, at least until Maria told her aunt. I know someone in Peyriac, near Marseilles, who promised he could cut some corners for us. It turned out he couldn't do a damn thing. Maria is an alien. She has to wait a year, some residence requirement. And that was that. We may try later in some other country. Or wait till I get to the States."

He met Conor's eyes.

"Did you know that Carrie was planning to take Maria home yesterday?"

There was complete silence. Conor's glance went past me.

"I didn't know," he said.

"Well," Egan said. He sucked in his breath, rose. "It's been a long day."

Maria jumped up and caught his hand, apprehension on her face. "Are you angry at me? I did have to keep it a secret for now but I would have written and explained. Nothing has changed for us, has it? I didn't even know myself why Carrie acted that way. It isn't what *I* want."

"Forget it, Maria," he said. "It doesn't matter now." His face was suddenly old and weary.

She still held his hand, going with him toward the stairs.

Conor didn't turn his head. He called, "Look in on Laure, will you? She isn't feeling well."

"Laure is here? Today?" His eyes hardened. "She's out of her mind."

"Even if she is, look in. Just as a gesture."

"She's your responsibility!" Egan flared again.

Conor's voice was deliberate. "It would be common courtesy."

"You could ask her how she's feeling, Egan," Maria spoke dully.

He dropped her hand, and went upstairs alone.

I put my arm around Maria, who looked as if her world had completely collapsed. "You could do with some sleep, too."

She let me lead her up the stairs. Ahead of us Egan was still impatiently knocking on Laure's door. It opened as we passed. Laure was in a disheveled negligee.

"So you're back, after worrying us all," she said. "What have you been up to, tricky bastard?"

She pronounced it in the English way, drawing out the first syllable, "baahstard," and laughing deep in her throat. Egan closed the door behind him.

Maria said, "Come into my room a minute, please? I'm tired, but I'll never sleep."

I sat on her bed while she pulled off her dress and let it lie on the floor and got into pajamas. Only when she stepped on the dress did she seem to notice it. She picked it up and mechanically put it on a hanger.

"It was my idea, honestly," she said. "Egan always said we should wait. He thought we should do it properly, with Aunt Millie there, but I knew it was the only way I could stay."

"Then you'll come home with me tomorrow?"

She shrugged. "I may as well, now."

There was a tap on the door, and Egan looked in. He stopped short; he hadn't expected to see me. He looked as drawn and taut as when Mlle. Sophie died.

"I want to speak to Maria," he said.

"I'm leaving," I said. "How is Laure?"

"Drunk. Or ill. Or crazy. Or all of them. She's mad to come when she knows how her husband feels about her being here."

So she had blurted her fears to Egan, too.

"She felt too shaky to drive home last night."

"Why didn't she hire someone in Belan to drive her?" he said curtly.

Why hadn't she? Because she hadn't thought of it?

"Do we have to talk about Laure?" Maria said in a small voice. "Especially since I'm going away tomorrow?"

"So you have definitely decided," he said to me.

"I think it's best," I said. "For everyone."

"It isn't best for Egan and me, is it, Egan?" She looked at him almost pleadingly. "It's all wrong for us!"

But he didn't answer as quickly as she needed him to.

"But maybe you're glad to see me go. Maybe all I've been is a nuisance to you." Her voice was trembling.

"No, Maria darling." He sat down at the edge of her bed, his face sharpened by exhaustion, his eyes defeated. He touched her hair, her cheek. "It's been a rotten summer, in too many ways. Carrie's unhappy, and wants to go home. You can't ask her to stay. We'll be together very soon, in New York, and we'll make up the time we've lost."

I couldn't bear the sound of defeat in his voice, I couldn't bear their misery. I thought of Romeo and Juliet. I felt like a bitch, coming between them. I muttered, "Good night. See you in the morning," and left them together.

I did not light the lamps in my room. I leaned against the window frame and for the last time breathed in that cold perfume of pine and lavender and wet leaves. I will never be whole again. Some part of me will stay behind here with Conor in his decaying hotel redolent of age and moldy stone, and sun and thin air and flowers. We will neither of us leave here unmarked, Maria or I.

They were going to let us go, then, Conor or Egan or whoever else had first tried to frighten us and then to kill me.

Maybe it would be simpler that way. We would make no trouble, three thousand miles away.

The heat of the day had given way to rain. I'd hardly heard the rain begin, it was so quiet, only a wet mist in the air, but now it was coming down harder, spattering on the terrace, the roof tiles. I shivered. The cold was penetrating. I should get into bed, but I knew I wouldn't sleep.

I thought of Laure. Drunk or crazy, Egan had said. Maybe she needed something. No, she was with Conor . . . But suppose she wasn't. Her window might be open, she might be too stupefied to close it. Maybe she could use something hot, some tea. If she was with Conor she would be in his room. I could tap on her door, and see. I was going down to the kitchen to make the tea for myself, anyway.

I went out into the darkened corridor and found her door, and knocked lightly.

"Come in."

She was sitting in a chair in her nightgown and robe, in the dark. I could hear the rain striking the glass of the long open windows.

"Laure. I was just going down to make myself some tea. Can I get some for you?"

"I'm very cold," she said.

I went to her windows and shut them. "Why don't you get into bed?"

She shook her head. I think her teeth were chattering. "I'm afraid to."

"Oh, Laure."

"My husband is going to kill me."

"You don't know what you're saying. Why don't you get into bed and I'll bring you the tea and that will help you sleep."

"I don't want to sleep. It will be easier for him if I am asleep."

"Why should he kill you? Because you stayed away from home for an extra two days? You're being foolish, Laure."

"He knows now," she said. "He knows I have been deceiving him." Her voice was thick. "Before, it was only Armad's word against mine. Now he will know."

"Armad?"

"He sent him to spy. I was so sure Armad would not guess. We were so careful. But he must have seen us."

I thought of Armad creeping up the tower steps after Laure, and I sat down at the foot of her bed, afraid. "But why should he kill you? There are other ways to rid yourself of an unfaithful wife. Divorce, for one. Aren't you being melodramatic, Laure?"

Her breath choked. "My husband is Turkish. You do not understand Turkish men. This is a matter of honor. In his country he will be freed for killing a faithless wife and her lover."

Her lover. Conor too would be killed. In my fear I cried out, "Then why did you come? Why did you disobey him?"

"You would not ask, if you loved. And knew you were losing him."

Losing him. Did she mean— Had Conor spoken to her of me? Is that why she was alone tonight?

"I am a fool," she said harshly, "but I had to come. I could not stay at the villa. I would have lost my mind. And now"— her laugh shattered—"I shall lose my life."

"You're overexcited, Laure. You don't know what you're saying."

"I telephoned Sarif. He would not speak to me. The ser-

vants said he had returned, I know he was there. I begged
them to tell him it was urgent, that I was ill, but he would
not answer the telephone." She rubbed her hands together, as
if to warm them. "I then called Armad. Anna answered.
Anna pitied me. She told me to go away from La Ferme, not
to let them find me here."

She must be speaking the truth. I cried, "Then why didn't
you go?"

"He would not come with me."

Because of me? I seized her hands. "You must make him!"

She shook her head. "I've pleaded. It's useless."

"Maybe he has no money—"

"I have money," she said bitterly. "More than enough. He
does not want to come with me. Do you understand?"

"You must tell him it's a question of life or death!"

"He will not come," she only repeated, dully.

"Speak to him again! Make him see how urgent it is!"

She shook her head.

"You have to go yourself, Laure," I said.

"I am too nervous to drive."

"I'll make you coffee. It will be better than tea. Have you
something warm to wear?"

I lit her lamp, pulled open the armoire doors. There was
the green suit she had come in. I flung it on her bed. "Get
dressed, Laure! I'll be back with the coffee in a few minutes."

I went down to the kitchen, the furious gusts of rain covering whatever sounds I had to make. I boiled the water and
put the coffee in the pot, spilling some in my haste.

Someone was standing in the doorway. I whirled around,
in panic. But it was Laure, still in her robe.

"Laure, why aren't you dressed?"

"I can't. I am trembling too much. I need some brandy."

"But you've had too much already."

"Brandy will steady me now."

Without lighting the lamps in the salon I made my way behind the bar and searched for the bottle of brandy. I found it, and poured some in a glass. She had followed me to the salon, and stood silhouetted against the long French doors.

"Here, Laure."

She did not move, and so I brought the glass to her. But when I tried to put it into her hand it was clenched into a claw. She pointed. I could not see anything, only her eyes glistening in terror.

"What is it?"

She tried to speak, but no sound came. I said again, "What is it? Tell me."

She managed a whisper. "He is here."

"Who?"

She breathed, "The assassin."

I saw him now myself, that heavyset body, the curiously female walk. Armad. He was darting across the courtyard to the front door.

I forced myself to speak calmly, though inwardly her terror gripped me. "It's only Armad. He isn't going to kill you. He's come to take you home. Your husband sent him for you."

Her teeth chattered. "Fool. My husband sent him to kill us both."

She and Conor. I managed to say, "How can he? Here, in a hotel full of people?"

"He will find a way. He has killed before, when my husband tells him."

"Laure, you're hysterical."

"He killed Sophie, because of what she guessed. He tried to kill you."

I breathed it: "Why?"

"You found the heroin. They were afraid."

"*They?*" But how did *they* know, unless Conor told them?

"Do you think it is one man?" she said. "It is many. Sarif, Armad, others—" Her voice broke to a whisper. "It is my lover. And I. Do you think it is only because we have betrayed my husband that we must die? It is because they are afraid we will betray them, too!"

The doorbell pealed.

She was moaning, "Don't answer the door. Bolt the windows—"

If he continued to ring, Conor might come down to answer it. The numbness of despair settled in me.

"Listen to me, Laure," I said. "You must take Conor and run. Use the back entrance. I'll keep Armad down here as long as I can."

She shook her head blindly. My fingers dug into her arms.

"Laure, you have to! It's the only way! Hurry! I don't know how long I can keep him with me!"

At least I galvanized her into movement. She seemed to see a desperate chance, and turned, and ran wildly toward the stairs. I clenched my nails into my palms until I finally heard a door open and close above me.

Conor had told Armad about my finding the heroin. The thought numbed my mind. I went to the door and pulled the bolt.

The assassin. Plump and squat, Armad smiled at me, his oily skin beaded with rain, his black hair streaked sparsely across his scalp.

"Carrie my dear, what a surprise! Did I wake you? I'm so sorry! I expected to see one of the servants."

"It's all right. I happened to be up making coffee."

Did I sound convincingly casual? I marveled at myself. It was Armad on the mountain. No taller than I was, my feet would have scraped the stone as he dragged me to the edge.

"May I come in?"

I stepped aside hurriedly. I hadn't been aware of blocking the doorway.

"The inn always has the welcome for the wayfarer, yes? It is not too late to have a bed?"

"The rooms aren't made up, but if you'll wait down here I'll fix up a bed for you myself." I was talking too fast, I would give myself away. "Can I give you some coffee while you wait? It's already made. I was just getting it for myself. You can have it here in the salon while I get your room ready. Wait, I'll turn on the lamps—"

"You are so agitated, Carrie," he said. "Where is the serene schoolmistress, so cool, so calm?"

"Well, you did frighten me, coming so late. The bell . . . Will you have coffee?"

"No coffee. A whiskey in my room, if you'll be so kind."

Numbly I went to the bar for the whiskey. "No coffee?"

He gestured implacably toward the stairs. "Just the bed, please. I am very tired. I do not like to drive under the most favorable of conditions and tonight it was dreadful, simply dreadful. If you will be so kind as to make up the bed, as you generously offered, please?"

I managed to remember to give him a room at the opposite end of the hall from Laure. I lit the lamp for him, and then I went to the linen cupboard for the sheets and towels, taking as long as possible. There was a thin crack of light under Laure's door, so she was still there. Had she called Conor yet? I could only hope she had.

I returned with the sheets.

Armad wagged his finger at me. "You would never find a place in my household as a chambermaid," he said to me. He had already poured some whiskey for himself, and was holding the glass in his hand.

"I'm sorry I'm so slow, but I didn't know which stack to use. Camille takes care of the linen."

I pulled back the spread with unnecessary care, and clumsily started to put the sheet on, tugging here, and pulling there, stalling for time. He put down his glass and came to the bed to help me, shaking his head at my ineptness.

"Laure is here," he said, a statement, not a question.

"She's asleep," I said. "She arrived here not feeling at all well, and she's been in her room most of the time."

"Poor Laure. Her nerves are very bad," he said.

"You should have come earlier," I said. "We had a beautiful hot day. What made you decide to come this late, and in such a storm?"

His black eyes surveyed me, narrowed, as I dawdled over the upper sheet. He took a sip of whiskey as if he were deliberating how to answer me.

"I came only as a special favor to my cousin, Sarif. He worries about Laure. He was afraid she might decide to come home in this rain."

"Why didn't he call?"

"Ah, the telephone. It was impossible to get through."

"She tried to call him today, to explain. She hasn't been well enough to travel."

"Poor Laure," he said. "Well, tomorrow we shall drive home together."

I folded and refolded the towels, putting them out first on the edge of the bed, then on the washstand.

"Dear Carrie," he said, "if you linger much longer I shall assume you wish to stay. Normally, you understand, there is nothing I would like more, but tonight I am very tired."

I know my face was burning. "I just wanted to make sure . . . everything . . ."

I got out.

I went to my room and stood behind the door listening. When I heard a sound from his room I opened my door a crack to see. But he was only crossing the hall to the bathroom. I waited in my darkened room until he had gone back to his.

Would he first see if she was with Conor? But I had told him that Laure was in her room all day ill. Did he believe me?

I had to make sure that they had gotten safely away. From my room I couldn't see the clearing for the cars. They would take her car, I was sure; it was faster than the old Citroën.

The only way to be sure they were gone was to go to her room. Again I opened a slit of door, and listened. No sound. I noticed with alarm that the dim light from the entry below managed to throw some illumination upward, enough maybe to make them afraid to chance crossing the corridor. I stole out and threw the switch at the head of the stairs, plunging the hall into total blackness. They would probably use the servants' stairway, and leave by the kitchen door.

But suppose she were still hiding in terror in her room, too panic-stricken to move, to rouse Conor.

I had to go to her room. The corridor was still. I ran down the hall and tried her door.

The room was dark.

"Laure?" I whispered.

The green suit was gone from her bed.

I almost cried out in my relief. I went to her window and leaned out. Even as I did, I saw their two figures, her blond head, his yellow slicker, emerge from the house and race across the clearing. So she had finally convinced him of the danger. I let out my breath.

They vanished under the trees. The rain buffeted the tiled roof, drowning out even the sound of a motor. But then I saw it, her pale-ivory-colored car rolling noiselessly over the cobbles. Someone had been clever enough to remember not to turn on the headlights, and if it weren't for the ivory color I might not even have seen it gliding toward the gates.

There was a faint sound behind me. I spun around. I could see nothing but a shape against the blackness of the hall, a short, squat shape. I caught my breath, and the gasp was loud even above the clattering of the rain.

"Is that you, Carrie?" he said.

I couldn't answer.

"Strange. I had expected Laure," he said.

Would he try to hurl me out of the window? No, it couldn't be explained as easily as the action of a mad old woman.

"I came to see how Laure was," I stammered. "But she . . . she seems to . . . not to be here."

"Perhaps she has recovered enough to travel," he said.

"I don't see . . . I mean, in this weather—"

"Ah, yes, this weather," he said. "It would be foolish to

travel in this weather. Especially with the brakes in her car—"

I leaned against the window frame. "The brakes? But she didn't say anything—"

"Sarif was very concerned," he said almost reproachfully. "It was why he urged her so forcefully not to come to La Ferme this time, at least not until she had the brakes repaired. The mechanic had warned her to have them fixed. But she is thoughtless, poor Laure. She was so anxious to come."

"She made it here all right on those brakes," I whispered.

"And used up whatever metal was left. I know. I checked them myself before I came in. Women are so foolish about mechanical matters. To take a chance on these roads. She might go a mile at most, and then—" He threw up his hands.

Sheer anguish blotted the fear from my mind. I lunged past him in such desperation that I must have caught him off guard, because he did not attempt to hold me back. Wrenching open the door I ran down the corridor to the black steps, rushing headlong down. I was outside, blinded by the pelting rain, running across the courtyard, drenched to my knees.

I could not see the car ahead of me, or even hear it. Maybe they had cut off the motor and were rolling, just as they had not turned on their headlights.

"Conor!"

How could they hear me, and would they even stop if they did? But I was beyond reason, sliding and slipping in a river of oozing mud, falling to my knees, clawing my way up and running again.

Suddenly, on one of the corkscrew turns below me, the headlights flashed on, and the motor roared. They imagined themselves safe, the car gathered momentum.

"Conor!" I screamed.

They were going too fast; the headlamps threw a wild pattern of light, from side to side in a crazy zigzag.

"Conor," I whispered, stopping, unable to run anymore.

I saw the car spin around even before I heard the sound of its falling, the terrible, grating, crashing sound. The white shape bounced and spun, metal cracking against rock, over and over, interminably, and then silence and darkness.

I stumbled forward blindly.

Arms seized me from behind. I struck out with my elbows fiercely. I no longer cared if he killed me—

"Carrie, for God's sake!"

The scream died in my throat.

Conor. I said his name again and again in disbelief, clinging to his drenched jacket.

"Then who is with Laure?"

But I knew by then.

"Egan," he said, his voice cracking. "Egan. It was always Egan."

VII

⌒

⌒

⌒

1

I CAN NEVER AGAIN BE THE GIRL I was before that night. Each detail is etched into me as corrosively as if by acid. I hear Laure's car catapulting down into the ravine with an almost human shriek. I hear the stillness, ponderous, tangible, when the car is crushed and silent. I still see that utter darkness. And then . . . those headlights coming at me through the rain like two vicious, yellow, inescapable eyes—

I held Conor until he put me away from him. "You must get back to the house, Carrie. Call the hospital and then the police. I'll go down to them."

I moved blindly, automatically, my head a chaos of images. That night we had come here, the incoherent babbling of Sophie about a quarrel. That must have been Laure and Egan, and she had run out to her car and he had gone after her, pleading with her to stay, but she had driven off in a jealous fury. She had been capable of that kind of jealousy, and Egan had known it, and had probably guessed it was

Laure who had slashed Maria's dresses, who had buried the blade in her soap. He had to cover for Laure, or disclose their relationship. She had not been capable of murder, poor Laure, only of that kind of rage which would have made her swerve at us that night, but not to drive us off the road to our death.

I went up to Camille's room and waked her, and warning her to silence I told her what had happened in the simplest way. She put on her robe and came down with me to the telephone and in a voice trembling with excitement at her role in the tragedy she phoned the police and the hospital. She wanted to dress and go with me, but I told her there was nothing for her to do, she might as well go back to bed and get her sleep. I ran up to my room for my raincoat, and when I came down there was Armad, beside the front door.

Incredible as it must seem, I had not thought of him. What had happened on the road had driven the image of the murderer from my mind. Now I stared at him, trying to comprehend him, curiously calm, curiously unafraid.

"A terrible tragedy," he said. "I have telephoned to my cousin, and he asks me to come and fetch him, and bring him here to his wife."

I said, "Murderer."

"My poor girl, you must be out of your mind."

I turned away.

"Her husband warned her not to drive. The mechanic at the garage warned her not to drive. The brakes were almost gone. Sarif called her from Istanbul, warning her again. Anna was there. Anna heard. So did the servants. Don't take the car into the mountains in its present condition, he said."

If the police investigated, they would bear him out, all of

them, the mechanic and the servants in Sarif's pay, Anna who had conveniently heard it.

"That poor young man," said Armad. "I am sure he only felt obliged to perform a service for a guest and friend, no matter how unreasonable, such as driving her home in this dreadful weather. Laure was such a faithful wife. She could not bear the thought that her husband had returned from Istanbul and she was not there to greet him. A rash, handsome boy, but with a good heart."

"The heroin. Do you imagine you will get away with that, too?"

"Heroin?" he said. "What heroin?"

The heroin was burned, the evidence destroyed.

"There is only you, Mlle. Carrie. Only your word."

There was nothing more to say. I opened the door. He gave me a little bow as I went out.

Once on the road I began to run. I should have taken a flashlight. When the lights of La Ferme disappeared behind the trees I had to move by instinct only. "Conor?" I called above the downpour. "Conor?" It must be farther down the road than I thought. Surely this bend was where I had last seen the car—

Headlights. I stopped, startled. They wavered through the trees, they vanished completely and reappeared closer. Now I could see the streaming furrows of mud in the road, the shape of the underbrush. The headlights crept closer like a yellow-eyed animal. The mountainside flashed beside me. Was that a white gleam of metal below?

"Conor?" I cried.

My mind must have been dull. It should not have taken this long, or was it so long, and did it not seem long only in

memory, and was it not only a matter of moments, really for
me to know that it would be Armad driving his car down the
mountain road from La Ferme? There is only you, Mlle
Carrie. *Only you.*

I turned, riveted, to stare at the oncoming lights. Now I
saw the car above, gathering speed. The headlights dazzled
my eyes and I lifted my hand to shield them, stupidly fixed to
that spot even as I realized that Armad had come after me,
had tracked me down. Who would question the circum-
stances, our minds clouded by shock and grief, the road im-
passable, the vision obscured, if I were run down on the road?

The headlights licked at me, faster, faster. Where could I
run to, even if my legs would carry me? On one side I would
be pinned to the sheer rock wall of the mountain, on the
other I would plummet down the slippery ravine to my
death.

"Carrie!"

I heard him call my name. I only vaguely saw Conor clam-
ber up to the level of the road. For an instant the headlights
picked him out, clear. Conor ran out in front of the car.

Brakes screeched, the headlights spun a wild arc. The car
careened, teetered, disappeared. I heard only the single dull
impact, and then a gaudy burst of color bloomed over the
mountains, flaming earth and rocks and branches, making the
rain a curtain of red gauze before it flickered and went out.

We stared down into blackness. The rain had extinguished
the flames quickly, and there was no sound from the car.

"He'll have to wait," said Conor, his voice hard.

He helped me down to where Laure's car lay. I did not
think yet, as I would later, how strangely, how justly, Conor
had effected a kind of retribution. Armad was a bad driver,

Laure always said that. He must have been momentarily disconcerted when Conor appeared before him, and lost control. I was only guessing, and how it happened seemed unimportant to me then.

Laure was dead, pinned behind the wheel, her long hair spilled across her face. Conor had pulled Egan clear, and put him down on a patch of sodden grass. He knelt beside him now, and pillowed his crushed head on his thigh. Egan was still alive.

I crouched down, and whispered his name. His eyes trembled and opened, but did not see me. He thought I was Maria.

He made a terrible effort to speak. "Mustn't . . . believe Laure."

Conor turned away, his face a relief of twisted stone.

"I won't believe her, Egan."

"We'll get married . . . New York," his wavering voice went on. "Only you . . . Maria . . . love." He was silent.

"I love you too," I said, as Maria would have said, and kissed his mouth, and wept, as she would have. When I think of that night, as I often do, I am grateful at least that he believed I was Maria.

We shielded his heedless face from the rain which fell relentlessly. The police van came first, and then the ambulance. Conor told someone about Armad's car. Men extricated Laure's broken body and wrapped it in canvas and stowed it away in the ambulance. When they lifted Egan onto the stretcher he was breathing harshly, and I saw the doctor turn to Conor and shake his head.

Conor went with Egan in the ambulance, and I walked back alone to La Ferme. When I passed the place where

Armad's car had fallen and burned I could still smell the acridness of flaming oil and charred metal, but as I went higher the air was cleaner, as if the rain had washed the smells away.

I paused in the doorway of La Ferme, enjoying the washed purity of the predawn air. I went inside, and the quiet seemed to follow me, as if the taint of evil were purged, and peace had come to the house. I sat down in the salon to wait for Conor.

The doctor dropped him off. I had made coffee, and brought it in.

"He died about an hour after we got him to the hospital."

The eerie, pearled light of a mountain dawn shifted and swirled outside the long windows and crept into the room.

"I never guessed he was involved with drugs. I suspected many things, not heroin. Even when you showed it to me, I didn't want to believe it was Egan. He had money, I knew, but when I asked him about it he'd say Laure gave it to him. I knew she was crazy about him. She would have died for him. She did."

The mists blotted out everything outside the windows, so the room seemed to float in a cloud. Only his words were harshly real.

"Her husband runs a reputable import business. It could serve as a façade for the drug traffic. Laure got Egan into it, I'm sure. Maybe she felt she could get a hold on him that way. He knew a lot of people in the States. He must have used them the way he did Maria, asking them to take packages for him to hold for other friends."

I thought of that first night I had met Miss Waldron, and

the man who had picked up the package there. Someone must have known about the operations of Laure and Sarif and Armad, and their confederates, someone who was watching the Waldron house. And then I thought of something else.

I said, "Was Egan just . . . using Maria, then?"

"Never believe that, Carrie. He loved Maria. If he hadn't loved Maria, he wouldn't be dead now. He was afraid to make an open break with Laure, with Maria coming. He was afraid she'd tell Maria about them. That's what he told me. I thought he was afraid Laure would tell Maria he'd been taking money from her. I didn't know it was his involvement with the heroin he was afraid she'd reveal. And she would have, even if it meant putting her life and her husband's in danger. She didn't give a damn about anything but Egan. Somehow Egan convinced her that this thing with Maria would be over after the summer, that he was only pretending so he could send stuff through her. She must have wanted to believe that badly. That's why she went along with the game that it was me she loved, not Egan."

"You went along with it, too."

"I had to. Egan was desperate. Maria was that important to him, and it was the least I could do for him. I knew it was a deadly game, and I was scared for him. I knew what Laure was like. I knew her husband was jealous. I've been frightened for their lives for a long time. I think he sent Armad to kill them not because they might talk but because she had defied him to come here to Egan."

He looked at me somberly. "How I hoped the two of you would never show up. How could I know it would be someone like you, and that I'd fall in love with you."

The words hung between us like a bridge, linking us.

"Laure wasn't a fool. She guessed how it was between Maria and Egan. She risked her husband's vengeance to come here and make one last try for Egan."

I didn't want to say it, but I had to. "Laure said it was Armad who killed Sophie. Who tried to kill me on the mountain. But it must have been Egan who called Armad."

"He was running scared. Of Sophie talking. Of you talking. He must have followed me when I burned the heroin. What drove him hardest was his fear Maria would find out."

It was dirty and ugly, his betraying us. But was it any uglier than the traffic he was engaged in?

Conor's face was haggard. He said, "He was amoral. He was unscrupulous. He was a coward. I didn't know how much, myself. Does it help any to know he suffered for it? Maybe he didn't have any conscience to stop him from doing what he did, but he had enough to make him suffer for it. When I held him tonight, he . . . he kept telling me that he was sorry." His voice faltered. He took a breath and went on, "It had to end this way. What was left for him? How could he ever be happy, even with Maria?"

I brought it up for the first time. "When you came out on the road tonight, in front of Armad's car—"

"I've been thinking of that, too," he said. "I'm not the kind of man who could kill, not to avenge, not for anything, but I'm glad I had something to do with his death, for Egan's sake."

We pressed close to each other for what comfort we could find. The mist outside thinned and turned coral and blew away. The buzzer sounded in the kitchen for the first break-fast tray. Camille looked in on us quietly and then went to the kitchen where we heard her clattering china and silver. Jeanne came down, and the vacuum hummed.

"You'll have to go away, at once," he said. "I'll wait until you're on the plane to talk to the police. At least they may get Sarif. My word against his, but I'll try."

We were silent. And then I said, "What will we tell Maria?"

Neither of us wanted to tarnish her memory of Egan. Conor said that once we were back in the States there was half a chance she might never hear of Egan's connection.

I left him, and went to my room and waited for her to wake. The news would keep, and she would learn it all too soon.

When she tapped on my door, I was surprised to see her dressed for travel.

"You did want to leave today," she said. "I've been thinking, the longer we stay the worse it will be. Egan was wonderful last night. You don't know him, Carrie, really. You don't know how sweet he can be. I'd almost want to leave without seeing him again, it was so perfect, just the way I remember it."

She saw my face.

"Don't feel badly, Carrie. I don't mind going. Not any more than you do, I guess. You don't really want to leave Conor either, do you? Carrie, you know something? If it'll make you feel any better, I don't really think Conor is that mad about Laure, not as much as Egan says he is—"

I had to break in.

"Maria, there's been a horrible accident. Laure is dead."

"Dead?" Her face was suddenly remote, her fingers played with her bracelet.

"She insisted on driving home in that storm last night."
We had agreed to use Armad's story; it salvaged as much as
was possible. "She was afraid of the roads alone, she didn't
feel well, and so—" But the words dried in my throat.

She whispered, "Was Conor with her?"

"Conor was asleep. Egan was still up—" I shut my eyes so I
would not have to see her face.

Her voice was light, a mere breath. "Not Egan, Carrie. Not
Egan."

She waited.

"Is he hurt?" she said. And then, "He's dead. That's right,
isn't it? He's dead."

I put my arms around her and held her. I was her friend, I
was her sister, I was her mother, I was all she had, and there
wasn't a word I could summon to help her.

"That horrible road," I muttered. "The brakes were bad.
Laure was so frightened. You know Egan. He felt sorry for
her and offered to drive—"

"He would do that," she said, her mouth against my shoulder. "He would do just that."

She never asked any questions about him. We packed the
car and drove away. I had said my real good-bye to Conor in
the salon, earlier. There was a plane that took us to Paris, and
then in Paris another that took us to New York. I have always
felt there was more to Maria than her pretty face suggested. I
think she already knew too much for her own happiness.

2

I did not write Miss Waldron until we reached New York,
and then all I put in my letter was that Egan had died in a

motor accident. I suggested that she should not prod Maria for details, but wait until she volunteered them herself. My role as chaperone to Maria was to determine the honesty of Egan's love for Maria; his death ended my part in their story.

For a week I stayed with Maria in the big house on Madison Avenue, because she didn't want to be alone with just the servants. But then I persuaded her to join her Aunt Millie in Seal Harbor. I was afraid I was a constant reminder of La Ferme.

Conor telephoned me when I returned to my loft. He had tried to reach me before, but for Maria's sake he did not want to call at her house, where he assumed I had gone. After that, things happened fast. I sent in my resignation to the Misses Burns, I sublet the loft, crated my paintings and sent them ahead, gave Peter what he wanted of my furnishings and sold the rest to the new tenants. Conor met me in Paris and we were married at the United States Consulate there.

Now I live at La Ferme. It would be a lie to say I can walk on that road, paved and fenced as it is now, and ignore the ghosts, but we are too happy for them to affect our lives. The hotel does well; *Guide Michelin* has awarded us a fork for our food, two peaked roofs for our accommodations and a squiggle for our exceptional location, and we've had offers from buyers, but we do not want to leave.

Maria writes now and then. She's been engaged several times but always breaks them off, so I know she is still under Egan's spell. But for the first she writes of visiting us this summer. To see the baby, she says, but maybe she is really testing herself. I think it's a good idea that she come. I think it will help her remember how wonderful it is to love.